PUFFIN BOOKS

Published by the Penguin Group
Penguin Books Ltd, 80 Strand, London WC2R 0RL, England
Penguin Group (USA) Inc., 375 Hudson Street, New York, New York 10014, USA
Penguin Group (Canada), 90 Eglinton Avenue East, Suite 700, Toronto, Ontario, Canada M4P 2Y3
(a division of Pearson Penguin Canada Inc.)
Penguin Ireland, 25 St Stephen's Green, Dublin 2, Ireland (a division of Penguin Books Ltd)
Penguin Group (Australia), 250 Camberwell Road, Camberwell, Victoria 3124, Australia
(a division of Pearson Australia Group Pty Ltd)
Penguin Books India Pvt Ltd, 11 Community Centre, Panchsheel Park, New Delhi - 110 017, India
Penguin Group (NZ), cnr Airborne and Rosedale Roads, Albany, Auckland 1310, New Zealand
(a division of Pearson New Zealand Ltd)
Penguin Books (South Africa) (Pty) Ltd, 24 Sturdee Avenue, Rosebank, Johannesburg 2196, South Africa

Penguin Books Ltd, Registered Offices: 80 Strand, London WC2R 0RL, England

penguin.com

Abridged from *The Magic Spell*. First published by Puffin Books 2002
Text copyright © Working Partners, 2002. Illustrations copyright © Biz Hull, 2002

Abridged from *Dreams Come True*. First published by Puffin Books 2002
Text copyright © Working Partners, 2002. Illustrations copyright © Biz Hull, 2002

Abridged from *Stronger Than Magic*. First published by Puffin Books 2003
Text copyright © Working Partners, 2003. Illustrations copyright © Biz Hull, 2003

Abridged from *A Special Friend*. First published by Puffin Books 2003
Text copyright © Working Partners, 2003. Illustrations copyright © Biz Hull, 2003

This collection of abridged stories first published in Puffin Books 2006

1

Text copyright © Working Partners Ltd 2006
Black and white illustrations copyright © Biz Hull 2006
Colour illustrations copyright © Andrew Farley 2006

Set in Bembo
Made and printed in China

British Library Cataloguing in Publication Data
A CIP catalogue record for this book is available from the British Library

ISBN-13: 978-0-141-38302–6
ISBN-10: 0-141-38302-X

My Secret Unicorn

The Secret Treasury

LINDA CHAPMAN

PUFFIN

Contents

The Magic Spell

Prologue

Deep in the mountains, mist swirled over a round stone table. A unicorn was standing beside it. With a snort, it lowered its noble head and touched the table's surface with its golden horn.

The table seemed to shiver for a moment. And then its surface began to shine like a mirror.

The unicorn murmured a name.

There was a flash of purple light and the mist cleared.

In the mirror, an image appeared. It was of a small grey pony.

Another unicorn came up to the table. It gazed at the grey pony thoughtfully. 'So, he is still looking for the right owner, to free his powers?' it said.

The golden-horned unicorn nodded its head. 'His last owner was often unkind.'

The other unicorn tossed its mane. Its silvery horn flashed in the light cast by the mirror. 'Surely, somewhere out there there must be someone who is good-hearted enough? Someone who has the imagination to believe in magic?'

'I think there is,' the golden-horned unicorn said softly. 'Watch. She is coming.'

Chapter One

'Where do you want this box, Mum?' Lauren Foster asked, staggering into the kitchen.

Her mum was kneeling on the floor, surrounded by packing cases. 'Just put it anywhere you can find a space, honey,' she said.

Lauren went over to the kitchen table and put the box on it. Just then, Max, her younger brother, came running in. Hot on his heels was Buddy, their ten-week-old Bernese mountain dog.

The puppy came bounding across the floor to say hello — and crashed straight into a stack of crockery that Mrs Foster had just unpacked. A couple of plates fell off the pile with a horrible clatter.

'Oh, Buddy . . .' Mrs Foster sighed.

'It's not his fault,' Max said. He rushed over to scoop the fluffy black and tan puppy into his arms. 'He just hasn't got the hang of stopping yet.'

Mrs Foster laughed.

Mr Foster, Lauren's dad, was directing the removal men, who were carrying furniture in from the removal lorry.

'What shall I do now, Dad?' Lauren asked. She dodged out of the way as one of the men marched past, carrying the family computer.

'Perhaps it would be best if you went and unpacked your bedroom, honey?' He hurried after the man with the computer. 'Please be careful! That's a delicate piece of equipment!'

Lauren grinned. It was a good idea to escape to her room!

It was strange to think that this house — Granger's Farm — was now her home. As she walked upstairs, Lauren thought about her two best friends back in the city, Carly and Anna. She wondered if they were missing her.

Feeling a little lonely, she walked along the landing to the bedroom at the far end and pushed open the white-painted wooden door. Her new room was small with a sloping ceiling. Sunlight streamed into the room through a little window.

Lauren stepped over the piles of boxes and suitcases and sat down on the window-seat to gaze at the view. The towering Blue Ridge Mountains in the distance were majestic and beautiful, but her eyes passed over them and fell on something much nearer to home: the little paddock and stable behind the house.

As she looked at them, her loneliness lifted. She might not know anyone here in the country but at least she was going to get a pony! A chance to have their own animals had been the first thing her parents had promised when they'd told her and Max about moving from the city. Max had chosen to have a puppy. They'd got Buddy a couple of weeks ago, and he was already a big part of the family. Everyone loved him. But for as long as Lauren could remember, she had wanted a pony of her own. And her mum was taking her to a horse and pony sale the very next day!

Lauren tried to imagine her pony. What colour would he be? How big? How old? Maybe he would be a black pony with four white socks, or a flashy chestnut, or a snow-white pony with a flowing mane and tail. Lauren smiled to herself. Yes, that's what she'd like – a beautiful white pony.

'Lauren!'

Lauren's eyes shot open. It was her mum, calling from the landing.

'I've unpacked some cookies,' her mum said. 'Why don't you come and have some with Max?'

'OK,' Lauren replied. And she went back down to join her family.

By the time Lauren went to bed that night, her bedroom was beginning to look more as if it belonged to her. Her clothes were hanging up in the closet and she had unpacked her books and cuddly toys.

Mrs Foster gently smoothed Lauren's hair. 'Time to get some sleep.'

Suddenly, Lauren didn't want to be left alone. This was the first night in their new home and it felt a bit strange. 'Will you read me a story, Mum?' she asked. Now that she was nine she didn't usually have a bedtime story. But this was an unusual night.

Her mum seemed to understand. 'Of course, honey,' she said. 'Which one do you want?'

'*The Little Pony*,' Lauren said, snuggling down beneath the duvet. *The Little Pony* was her favourite story. Mrs Foster was a writer and she'd written the story especially for Lauren when Lauren was just three years old. It was about a little white pony who travelled the world trying to find a home. He had almost given up when, one day, he met a girl who became his friend. And from then on, they'd looked after each other.

Her mum sat down on the bed and opened the book. As always, she started at the very first page. 'To Lauren, my very own little girl,' she read out softly.

Lauren shut her eyes and smiled at the familiar, comforting words of the story. Halfway between wakefulness and sleep, plans for the next day went round in her head. They were going to a horse and pony sale! *This time tomorrow*, she thought, *I'll have a pony of my own*.

Chapter Two

Soon after breakfast, Lauren set off with her mother for the sale. They left Max and her father at home with Buddy.

Even though it was raining, the parking area was already very busy when they arrived. Horses were being led about and the air was filled with shouts and whinnies. Loose dogs darted in between people's legs. Stable-hands dashed around with grooming brushes and saddles.

Lauren felt very excited. 'Where do we go?' she asked.

Her mum pointed out a sign that said LIVESTOCK. 'The horses and ponies will be over there.'

Lauren followed her mum through the crowds until they came to a large covered ring.

A bay horse was being trotted around the ring by a stable-hand. A man standing on a platform at one end was calling out a price, raising his voice above the noise of the rain drumming on the roof. 'One thousand, two hundred dollars I'm bid. Do I have any advance on one thousand, two hundred?'

A woman near Lauren held up her hand.

The man nodded at her. 'One thousand, three hundred to the lady on my left. Any advance on one thousand, three hundred dollars?'

Lauren turned to her mum. 'So the person who offers the most money gets the horse?'

Her mum nodded. 'The auctioneer – that's the man on the platform – keeps raising the price until no one else bids.'

'Any advance on one thousand, three hundred?' the auctioneer shouted. No one moved. He raised a small wooden hammer. 'Going, going – gone!' he said, bringing the hammer down on the table beside him with a bang. 'Sold to the lady on my left.'

The lady smiled and the horse was led out of the ring.

'Come on, let's go and look around,' Mrs Foster said to Lauren. She led the way towards an enormous barn beside the ring. Lauren gasped when she looked inside. It was full of pens and nearly all had horses standing in them. There were bays and chestnuts and greys, each awaiting their turn in the ring. Lauren thought they all looked very big.

Lauren's mother had disappeared ahead of her through a gate, but Lauren didn't want to walk too quickly; she didn't want to miss a thing. Carefully she picked her way through the puddles underfoot and made her way through the crowd. She reached the gate at the same time as an elderly lady who was sheltering beneath a brightly coloured umbrella. Lauren held the gate open for her.

The lady nodded. 'Thank you,' she said.

Lauren followed her through. The lady suddenly slipped on the wet ground and almost fell. 'Careful!' Lauren cried. She reached forward to hold the lady's elbow until she had regained her balance.

'Thank you again,' the lady said, her face creasing into a wide smile. She had the friendliest blue eyes that Lauren had ever seen.

'You're welcome,' Lauren said, smiling. 'I'm Lauren,' she went on.

'Hello, Lauren,' the lady answered. 'So if you're here at the sale, I guess you like ponies.'

Lauren nodded. 'I love them! My parents are going to buy me one.' She didn't want to sound spoilt, but she couldn't stop herself from blurting out her amazing news.

'Aren't you lucky?' The lady's eyes twinkled as they met Lauren's.

'I'm the luckiest person in the world,' Lauren breathed. 'Will you be OK now? I ought to get going. My mother will be wondering where I am.'

'I'll be just fine, thank you,' the lady replied. 'I hope you find the pony you're looking for.'

'There you are, Lauren!' her mother exclaimed.

'I thought I'd lost you.'

'Not a chance,' Lauren grinned. She looked excitedly at the ponies in front of her.

In the first pen, there was a tiny black pony. The next pen was empty, but beside it there were two pretty chestnuts with matching white stars. Next to them was an old grey mare with feathery legs and a large head, and beside her was a cheeky-looking bay. On the door of each pen there was a card with details about the pony inside.

There was no sparkling white pony like Lauren had been imagining, but she didn't care. 'They're all lovely!' she gasped, turning around to her mum.

'Well, this one's much too small,' Mrs Foster said, as she looked at the little black pony. 'We want a pony who's about thirteen hands high and at least six years old. Any younger and he'll be too inexperienced.'

Lauren ran over to the bay gelding's pen and looked at the card attached to his gate. 'Topper,' she read out. 'Thirteen hands. Four years old.' She felt a flicker of disappointment. He was too young. She patted him and moved on.

The grey mare was too tall, the black pony was too small, and the chestnut ponies were only three years old. Lauren walked along the line of ponies, reading their sale notices. She reached the end of the row. Not one of them was right.

Her mum came up behind her and squeezed her shoulder. 'Maybe we won't find your perfect pony today. We can always come to the next sale. It's only a month away.'

A month! Lauren couldn't wait that long.

Just then, she heard the sound of hooves. She swung around. A man was leading a scruffy grey pony out of the vet's tent and down the walkway towards the last empty pen. 'I thought I wasn't going to get here in time for the sale,' he said, noticing Lauren and her mum.

The pony looked quiet and sad.

'Hi, boy,' Lauren said, going over to him.

At the sound of her voice, the pony lifted his head and pricked his ears. He whinnied and Lauren felt her heart flip. Suddenly she didn't care that he was scruffy and dirty. This was the pony she wanted. 'How old is he?' she asked the pony's owner.

'Twilight? He's seven,' the man replied.

Lauren swung around to her mum. 'He's the right age!' The pony stepped forward and thrust his nose into her hands. His breath was warm as he nuzzled at her fingers.

'Can we buy him?' Lauren asked her mother eagerly.

The man smiled at them. 'Are you looking for a pony?'

'Yes, we are,' Mrs Foster replied. She walked forward and looked at Twilight. Why's he for sale, Mr – ?'

'Roberts – Cliff Roberts,' the man said, introducing himself and shaking hands. 'The pony's for sale because my daughter, Jade, doesn't want him any more,' he explained. 'I only bought Twilight for her a few months ago but she says he's too quiet and not showy enough. I've just bought her a new pony to take to shows, so now I've got to sell Twilight.'

'Can we buy him?' Lauren asked her mum again.

'Well, you'll have to have a ride on him first,' her mum said. She turned to Twilight's owner. 'Would that be possible, Mr Roberts?'

Mr Roberts smiled. 'Of course. It looks like the rain has stopped now. I'll just go and get the saddle.'

Five minutes later Lauren found herself riding Twilight around the exercise paddock. He felt wonderful. The slightest squeeze of her legs made him go faster and the smallest pull on the reins slowed him down. It was almost as though he could read her mind.

'That's amazing!' Mr Roberts said, as Lauren brought Twilight to a halt by the paddock gate and dismounted. 'He hardly wanted to do anything for Jade. He must like you.'

'I love him!' Lauren said, her eyes shining. She stretched out her hands towards Twilight. The pony lowered his muzzle and blew softly on Lauren's face. 'Please can we buy him?' she begged her mother. 'He's perfect!'

'He certainly seems very well behaved,' Mrs Foster said, patting Twilight. 'Maybe we'll bid for him when he goes into the ring.'

Lauren thought about the sale and the way the person who offered the most money got the pony. 'But someone else might bid more than us,' she said in alarm. 'Can't we just buy him now?'

'I'm quite happy to arrange a private sale, if you're interested,' Mr Roberts said to Lauren's mother. 'I wouldn't have to pay the auction fee then, so it would save me some money. How about we say . . .' He thought for a moment and then named a price. 'I'll even throw in the saddle and bridle if you like.'

Lauren looked at her mum and crossed her fingers. She didn't think she could bear to see Twilight go into the ring and be sold to someone else. *Oh, please*, she prayed. *Please say yes.*

To her amazement, her mum smiled. 'OK, Mr Roberts. You've got yourself a deal.'

Lauren could hardly believe it. She threw her arms round Twilight's neck and hugged him. 'Oh, Twilight!' she gasped in delight. 'You're going to be mine!'

The little grey pony nuzzled her happily, as if he understood.

Chapter Three

It was soon arranged that Mr Roberts would drive Twilight round to Granger's Farm the next morning.

On the way home Lauren and her mum drove to the local tack store on the outskirts of the town.

The sales assistant, a girl called Jenny, was very helpful. Soon there were loads of horsy things on the counter – brushes, a first-aid kit, feed buckets, a head-collar. The pile grew bigger and bigger until, at last, Lauren had everything she needed.

Jenny helped them pack all their purchases into their car. 'Have fun with your new pony!' she called to Lauren.

Lauren grinned at her. 'Thanks! I will!'

As Jenny went back to the store, Lauren noticed a small bookshop tucked between the tack store and a shop selling electrical goods. It had an old-fashioned brown and gold sign over the window saying MRS FONTANA'S NEW AND USED BOOKS. 'Look at that bookshop, Mum,' she said.

'Shall we take a look inside?' Mrs Foster asked.

Lauren nodded eagerly. Both she and her mum loved bookshops, and this one looked really interesting.

They walked along the pavement. Through the glass panel in the door, Lauren could see a cheerful rose-patterned carpet, and shelves and shelves of books.

Mrs Foster pushed the door open. A bell tinkled and they stepped inside.

'Wow!' Lauren said, looking around. There were books everywhere!

Just then there was a pattering of feet, and a little white terrier dog with a black patch over one eye came trotting up to them.

'Look, Mum!' Lauren exclaimed. She crouched down and the terrier licked her hand.

'Isn't he cute?' said Lauren.

'Ah, I see you've met Walter.'

Lauren and her mum looked up. An elderly lady was coming towards them. Lauren gasped. It was the lady she'd met at the horse sale earlier! There was no mistaking the warm blue eyes.

'Hello, Lauren,' the lady said, smiling.

'You two know each other?' Lauren's mother said, looking surprised.

'We met at the horse and pony sale this morning,' the lady explained. She held out her hand. 'I'm Mrs Fontana,' she said. 'This is my shop.'

'Alice Foster,' Lauren's mum said, shaking hands. 'We've just moved into the area. Is it OK if we have a look around?'

'Feel free,' Mrs Fontana replied. She smiled at Lauren. 'There are lots of books in the side room you might like.'

Leaving her mum to browse, Lauren made her way to the side of the shop. The next room was full of children's books. There were no bright posters or colourful displays like there were in most bookshops, but there were lots of plump, soft cushions on the floor and a big table piled high with all kinds of books.

Lauren examined each pile and quickly picked out a collection of pony stories. She sat down on one of the cushions and started to read.

Suddenly she heard the patter of paws coming towards her.

It was Walter, the terrier. He sat down beside Lauren and looked at her, his head cocked on one side. Lauren tickled him under the chin.

'He likes you,' Mrs Fontana said.

21

Lauren jumped. The old lady seemed to have appeared out of nowhere.

She smiled again at Lauren. 'Did you find your pony at the sale today?'

'I certainly did,' Lauren said, nodding excitedly. 'He's called Twilight and he's wonderful!'

Mrs Fontana stared at her for a moment and then she swung around. 'You know what?' she said. 'I think I might have just the thing for you.'

Lauren watched as Mrs Fontana pulled out a dusty purple book. She handed the book to Lauren.

Lauren looked at the words on the cover. '*The Life of a Unicorn*,' she read out.

She opened the book. The pages were smooth and yellow with age. There was lots of writing, but also some beautiful pictures. Unicorns cantered in the sky and grazed on soft grass. 'They're lovely,' she said as she turned the pages.

'Yes,' Mrs Fontana agreed, sighing.

Lauren stopped at the next picture. There was no unicorn to be seen, just a small grey pony.

'That's a young unicorn,' Mrs Fontana said, looking over her shoulder.

'But it hasn't got a horn,' Lauren said.

'Ah, but, you see, young unicorns don't have horns,' Mrs Fontana told her. 'They only grow their horns and receive their magical powers when they hear some magic words on their second birthday. Then they turn into the creatures that we know as unicorns.'

Lauren looked at her in surprise. From the way Mrs Fontana was talking, she made it sound as if unicorns were real.

'But unicorns don't really exist, do they?' Lauren said to the old lady. 'They're just made up, like fairies and dragons and trolls.'

'You don't think fairies, dragons and trolls exist either?' Mrs Fontana said, raising her eyebrows.

'No way,' Lauren grinned.

'Why not?' Mrs Fontana said.

Looking into Mrs Fontana's blue eyes, Lauren suddenly felt less certain. 'Well, no one has ever seen them,' she faltered.

'Maybe that's because they don't want to be seen,' Mrs Fontana said. 'Shall I tell you a secret? I've seen a unicorn.'

Lauren stared at her in astonishment. Had Mrs Fontana gone crazy?

Mrs Fontana seemed to read her mind. 'Oh, I'm not mad, dear,' she said with a smile. 'All it needs are the magic words, spoken by the right person, a handful of the secret flowers – and a unicorn, of course.'

Just then there was the sound of footsteps. 'Are you ready, honey?' Mrs Foster asked. 'We should be going home.'

Mrs Fontana straightened up briskly. Lauren felt as if she had been jerked out of a dream.

'What's that?' her mum said, seeing the book in Lauren's hands.

'A . . . a book on unicorns,' Lauren said, standing up.

Mrs Foster glanced at the book. She took in the soft leather binding and the pictures, glowing in jewel colours. 'It looks very expensive, honey. I'm afraid we can't afford it,' she said.

Lauren nodded. She hadn't really expected her mum to buy it for her.

'I'd like you to have it,' Mrs Fontana said softly.

Lauren looked at her in amazement.

The old lady smiled. 'Think of it as a gift to welcome you to the town.'

'But, Mrs Fontana, that's much too generous . . .' Mrs Foster began.

'Not at all,' said Mrs Fontana. 'It's a very special book and it needs a good home. Something tells me that Lauren will look after it.'

'Oh, I will!' Lauren gasped. 'Thank you, Mrs Fontana.' She took the book in her hands and held it close to her.

The bookshop owner showed them to the door. 'Do call again,' she said. 'And good luck at Granger's Farm.'

'We will – and thank you so much for the welcome gift,' Mrs Foster said.

The door tinkled shut behind them. Lauren was suddenly struck by a thought. 'How did Mrs Fontana know that we had moved to Granger's Farm? We didn't tell her.'

Mrs Foster frowned. 'Didn't we?'

'No,' Lauren said.

Her mum shrugged. 'Oh, well, it's a small town. News has probably got around. Now, come on. Dad and Max will be wondering where we are.'

Chapter Four

As Mrs Foster drove back to Granger's Farm, Lauren looked at the beautiful book she had been given. When she came to the page with the picture of the baby unicorn, she could almost hear Mrs Fontana's voice saying, *I've seen a unicorn.*

Lauren gently stroked the picture with her fingertip. She was sure that Mrs Fontana must have been making up all that stuff about magical creatures. The old lady couldn't really have seen a unicorn.

Could she?

Of course she couldn't, Lauren told herself firmly. *Unicorns don't exist. Mrs Fontana has just been reading one too many of her old books.*

That night, when Lauren went to bed, she opened the book that Mrs Fontana had given her and began to read the first chapter. '*Noah and the unicorns,*' she whispered quietly to herself . . .

Many years ago, there was a great flood that threatened both animals and magical creatures. The magical creatures fled to safety in Arcadia, an enchanted land that can't be found by humans.

Meanwhile, a man called Noah gathered together two of every animal and took them on to the Ark he had built. As the rain started to fall, Noah saw two small grey ponies in the grassy meadows beside the rising sea. He took them on to his Ark with the rest of the animals.

Through a magic mirror, the unicorns in Arcadia watched gratefully as Noah took care of their young. For these two grey ponies were, in fact, baby unicorns who hadn't yet grown into their magical powers. They had been left behind in the rush to Arcadia.

Whilst on the Ark, the time for the two young unicorns to gain their magical powers came and went. They had lost their chance. And the unicorns in Arcadia mourned.

When a whole year had passed, the floods went down. Noah released the young unicorns on to the Earth with the other animals. And there they remained, trapped in their pony bodies.

Back in Arcadia, the watching unicorns worked on a Turning Spell that would give the unicorns another chance to gain their magical powers. The spell took years and years to perfect. At last it was ready. But the spell would only free a unicorn if spoken by a good-hearted human who believed in magic.

A very brave unicorn risked his own powers to fly back to Earth. He searched long and hard for a human to whom he could entrust the spell.

Eventually he found her. The spell worked – and the two young unicorns became great friends with the human who had helped them. They grew beautiful horns and flew like angels. And together they had many magical adventures . . .

Chapter Five

Lauren put the book down. The way the book was written made everything about unicorns sound so real, not like a made-up story at all. She looked at the picture at the end of the chapter. It showed a beautiful unicorn cantering up into the sky.

I wish the story was true, Lauren thought. *I wish there were still unicorns on the Earth. I'd love to help one.*

And then she smiled. Unicorns might not exist, but Twilight did and he was going to arrive the very next day.

Mr Roberts arrived with Twilight at ten o'clock. He opened the side door of the trailer so that Lauren could get inside. Twilight whinnied as she stepped into the trailer.

'Hello, little one,' Lauren said, stroking his nose.

Twilight looked at her. *Hello,* his dark eyes seemed to say back.

Mr Roberts lowered the ramp to the ground. 'You can bring him out now, Lauren!' he called.

Lauren untied Twilight and backed carefully out of the trailer. Her mum and dad and Max came over.

'Hello, boy,' Mrs Foster said, feeding Twilight a carrot.

'He's really dirty, isn't he?' Max said, as he patted Twilight and a cloud of dust flew into the air.

Twilight whinnied indignantly, as if he understood what Max had said.

Mr Roberts smiled ruefully. 'I'm afraid my daughter has been busy with her new pony. She hasn't been looking after Twilight as well as she might.' He looked at Lauren. 'You'd like Jade. She's just crazy about ponies.'

Lauren wasn't so sure. If Mr Roberts's daughter was really crazy about ponies, she would have looked after Twilight better. But she didn't say anything.

While Mr and Mrs Foster sorted out paying Mr Roberts, Lauren and Max led Twilight to his stable.

'Are you going to ride now, Lauren?' Max asked.

'I'm going to groom him first,' Lauren replied.

She tied Twilight up outside the stable and fetched the grooming kit. 'Can I help?' asked Max.

'OK,' Lauren said, handing him a brush with thick bristles called a dandy brush. It was good for getting rid of dirt and dust. 'You can brush him with that.' Twilight nuzzled her shoulder. Lauren smiled happily and kissed his face. She didn't think she'd ever felt happier in her life.

Two hours later, Twilight was looking much smarter. The dust had come out of his coat and Lauren had replaced the old, tatty head-collar he had been wearing with the new red and blue one that she and her mum had bought the day before. However, despite everything, Twilight still looked a bit scruffy. Still, Lauren didn't mind.

With her mum's help, Lauren tacked Twilight up and rode him into the paddock. Just like the day before, he seemed to know exactly what she wanted him to do, and soon they were cantering around the field. When Lauren finally stopped him by the gate, her face was flushed and her eyes were shining. 'He's just great!' she said to her mum. 'Can I go for a ride in the woods?' She saw her mum look doubtful. 'I won't go far.'

'OK,' Mrs Foster agreed. 'But don't stay out too long.'

'I won't, I promise,' Lauren said. She remounted and rode Twilight out of the paddock. The mountain that rose up behind the farmhouse was thickly wooded and, as she rode Twilight into the trees, she felt his ears prick and his step quicken.

Lauren smiled happily. 'You like it up here, don't you, boy?'
Twilight snorted and broke into a trot.

Lauren let him have his head and he broke into a canter. They
made their way along the trail. The air was quiet so that the only sound,
apart from the thudding of Twilight's hooves on the soft ground, was
the distant calling of birds in the tops of the trees. Lauren felt that she
could have gone on forever. But she remembered what she had promised her mum, so she slowed Twilight down to turn him around.

Twilight looked to one side. A small side-trail led off the main
track. He pulled towards it. Lauren stopped him. 'No,' she told him.
'We've got to go back now.' Twilight pulled towards the side-trail again.

'We'll go another day,' Lauren told him and then, turning him
around, she rode back to the farm.

★

That night, when Lauren went to bed, she opened the unicorn book to a beautiful picture showing unicorns grazing in lush meadows dotted with star-shaped purple flowers. The pink sky was streaked across with orange and gold, as if the sun was setting. She began to read . . .

When the two young unicorns grew old they returned to Arcadia. The unicorn elders decided that from then on they would send young unicorns to Earth to do good works. They look like small ponies. Each of them hopes to find someone who will learn how to free their magical powers. To do this one needs: the words of the Turning Spell, a hair from the unicorn's mane, the petals from a single moonflower and the light of the Twilight Star, which only shines for ten minutes after the sun has set.

Lauren turned the page and saw the picture of the young unicorn that she had seen in Mrs Fontana's shop. Scruffy and grey, it looked quite like Twilight.

Maybe Twilight's a unicorn in disguise, Lauren thought suddenly.

She smiled to herself. She was being silly. It was just a made-up story and Twilight was just a regular pony.

Chapter Six

After breakfast the next morning, Lauren took Twilight out for a ride in the woods again. It felt a bit lonely on her own. *I wish I had someone else to ride with*, she thought. She wondered if she would make friends with someone when school started.

As they reached the trees, Twilight pricked up his ears and pulled at the reins.

'OK, boy,' Lauren said, letting him trot.

She had been riding for ten minutes when Twilight suddenly stopped.

'Go on!' Lauren encouraged him.

But Twilight wouldn't move. He shook his head and looked to the left.

Lauren realized that he was looking along the same side-trail he had tried to go down the last time they had been in the woods. She thought for a moment. What harm could there be in exploring?

'All right,' she said, turning Twilight towards it.

The track was narrow and the trees on either side met over Lauren's head, blocking out the sun. It was like riding through a long, green tunnel.

'Maybe we should turn back,' she whispered to Twilight, but the pony pulled eagerly on the reins. It was clear he didn't want to stop.

Lauren saw light ahead. It looked as if the track was coming to an end.

Wondering where they would come out, she let Twilight carry on. He trotted out from among the trees and into a grassy glade.

It was beautiful. In the centre of the glade there was a mound dotted with purple flowers where a cloud of yellow butterflies fluttered in the sunlight.

Twilight walked to the mound and Lauren saw that the flowers were star-shaped and at the tip of each bright petal there was a golden spot. She frowned. She knew she had seen them somewhere before, but she couldn't remember where. Now Twilight was nuzzling at the star-shaped flowers. Her curiosity was aroused and she dismounted.

Looping the reins round her arm, she looked closely at the flowers. Where *had* she seen them before?

Twilight whickered and nudged her arm. Lauren was puzzled. It was as if he was trying to tell her something, she thought, then she shook her head.

He's just a pony, she reminded herself quickly.

She glanced around. The glade was so beautiful and still that she didn't want to leave. But she knew that she ought to be getting home, so she mounted Twilight and rode him back into the trees.

Lauren turned Twilight on to the main trail through the woods where the birds were singing overhead again. Leaning forward, she let him go faster and they cantered along the track towards home.

When they got back to the farm, Lauren went into the study, where her dad had loads of books about plants. She took the biggest one down from the shelf and began to look through the section on woodland flowers. But she couldn't find any flowers that looked like the ones in the glade.

'I thought I heard you in here,' Mrs Foster said, coming into the study. 'What are you doing?'

'I've been trying to find the name of some flowers I saw in the woods,' Lauren replied. 'They were purple, sort of star-shaped with a gold spot at the tip of each petal.'

'Sorry, I can't help you,' her mum said. 'They sound very unusual, though. Now,' she went on, changing the subject, 'we need to get you some things for school – you start next week. Why don't you run upstairs and get changed and we'll go to the mall?'

'OK,' Lauren said.

She hurried up to her room and pulled on a pair of clean jeans and a sweatshirt. The unicorn book was lying on her bedside table. It was still open at the picture of the unicorns grazing. She glanced at it again: the unicorns, the grassy meadows, the purple flowers . . .

The purple flowers!

She stared at the picture. They were exactly the same as the ones she had just seen in the wood!

Chapter Seven

Lauren snatched up the book. The flowers in the picture had the same star shape, the same gold spot. A wild thought filled her mind. The book had said that unicorns disguised as ponies could be changed back by saying a magic spell and using a certain type of flower. What if the flowers she had found in the wood were the very ones that were needed in the spell?

She quickly turned the pages of the book until she found the part that explained how unicorns disguised as ponies could be changed back into unicorns. In the middle of the page there was a small picture of a purple flower just like the ones in the wood. Lauren read the words under the picture.

The moonflower: a rare purple-flowering herb that is used in the Turning Spell.

Lauren stared. She'd found the flower that the book said could give a unicorn its magical powers. She remembered the way Twilight had been nuzzling at the flowers in the glade. Maybe the story was true . . . and maybe, just maybe, Twilight really was a unicorn in disguise!

Her heart started to race. If she could just find the words of the spell, then she could try it out.

'Lauren! Are you coming?' her mum called.

Lauren could hardly bear to put the book down. The spell had to be here somewhere.

'Lauren!' her mum called again.

Lauren closed the book reluctantly. 'I'm coming!' she called, and she went downstairs.

★

Normally Lauren loved buying things for a new school term, but not that day. All she could think about was unicorns.

On the way home, Mrs Foster stopped by the tack store to pick up a couple of spare feed buckets.

Lauren had an idea. 'Can I go and look in the bookshop?' she asked.

'Sure,' Mrs Foster agreed. 'I'll meet you there in a few minutes.'

Lauren ran to the bookshop. The doorbell tinkled as she went inside. She caught sight of the owner near the back of the shop. 'Mrs Fontana!' she called.

The old lady turned around. 'Hello, dear,' she said. 'What can I do for you?'

Suddenly Lauren didn't know what to say. Mrs Fontana looked so calm and ordinary that the whole idea of asking her if she knew what the magic spell was seemed really dumb. 'Um . . . well . . . I . . .' Lauren stammered.

'So, have you seen a unicorn yet?' Mrs Fontana said softly.

Lauren stopped stammering and stared.

'That's what you wanted to talk to me about, isn't it?'

Lauren didn't even stop to ask how the old lady knew. 'Is the story really true?' she gasped.

Mrs Fontana smiled. 'It's true for those who want it to be true.'

'Do you know what the spell is?' Lauren asked eagerly.

'I do, but I can't tell you,' the old lady replied. 'Those who want to find unicorns must do it for themselves. You have everything you need.'

'But . . .' Lauren began.

Just then Walter gave a warning

bark. The shop door swung open and Lauren's mum came in. 'Hello, Mrs Fontana,' she said.

'Hello,' the bookshop owner said with a smile. 'So how are you settling in at Granger's Farm?' Her tone changed and now she sounded brisk and efficient.

Lauren waited while the two adults chatted. She longed to ask the bookshop owner more, but she couldn't with her mum standing there.

Lauren thought about the old lady's words: *You have everything you need.*

What did she mean?

That night, when she went to bed, Lauren decided to read the book from the beginning through to the end.

Starting at the first chapter, she read that after the floods had gone down, the magical creatures decided not to live on Earth any more and stayed in Arcadia. Arcadia was ruled by seven Golden Unicorns who watched the Earth through a magic mirror.

Lauren read on, but she didn't find the spell.

She awoke the following morning to see the book lying beside her on her bed. She had just two chapters left to read. She wondered whether to start on them, but then she saw that it was seven o'clock. It was time to get up and give Twilight his breakfast. She took the book outside with her. She could read it while he was eating.

Quickly, Lauren emptied the feed into the manger. She sat down on an upturned bucket and began to read. Surely the spell had to be in the book somewhere!

Lauren became aware that Twilight had stopped eating. He was staring at the book. With a snort, he walked over to her.

'Hello, boy,' she said.

Twilight blew gently. The pages of the book fluttered over.

'Twilight! You've lost my place!' Lauren said. But before she could turn back to the page she had been reading, Twilight breathed out again.

'What are you doing?' Lauren asked, as he nuzzled his soft lips against the back cover. They left a damp mark on the paper and she made to push his muzzle away but, as she did so, she realized that the last page of the book had been glued to the back cover. One corner of the page fluttered slightly as Twilight breathed on the book.

Lauren carefully pulled at it. The glue gave way and the page turned.

Inside the cover were some faint words written in pencil. It looked like a poem of some sort. Lauren read the title: *The Turning Spell.*

Chapter Eight

Trembling with excitement, Lauren read the faintly pencilled words:

'Twilight Star, Twilight Star,
Twinkling high above so far.
Shining light, shining bright,
Will you grant my wish tonight?
Let my little horse forlorn
Be at last a unicorn!'

Her eyes flew to Twilight. 'Oh, Twilight,' she whispered. 'It's the spell!'

Twilight bent his head as if he was nodding.

Lauren jumped to her feet. She had to take Twilight to the woods and pick one of those flowers!

After giving Twilight time to digest his breakfast, Lauren tacked him up and rode into the woods. Twilight seemed to know just where they were going.

They turned down the narrow track and followed it until they reached the sunny glade.

Lauren dismounted and led Twilight over to the grassy mound, where she found a single purple flower that had fallen to the ground. She picked it up. As she did so, a sharp tingle ran down her spine.

She felt Twilight's warm breath on her shoulder and she looked at him. 'Oh, Twilight,' she whispered. 'I hope this is going to work.'

'Dad, what time does the sun set?' Lauren asked her father that afternoon. Her book had said that the Twilight Star only shone for ten minutes after the sun had set and that the spell had to be performed then.

'About seven o'clock at the moment,' her dad said. 'Why?'

'I just wondered,' Lauren said quickly.

At six-thirty her mum put supper out.

Lauren ate as fast as she could. 'May I leave the table, please?' she asked as soon as her plate was empty.

Her mum looked surprised. 'You know better, Lauren – not till everyone's finished,' she said.

So Lauren had to wait. Through the kitchen window she watched the sun dropping lower and lower in the sky. She was going to miss the sunset!

At long last her dad put his knife and fork down. 'That was delicious,' he said.

Before he had even finished speaking, Lauren had jumped to her feet. 'Can I go and see Twilight now, Mum?' she begged.

'All right,' Mrs Foster said. 'Go on.'

Lauren grabbed her jacket and ran out of the door. The book was still in Twilight's stall. She fetched it and raced down to the paddock. Her heart was pounding in her chest. What would happen? Would the spell really work?

Twilight was standing by the gate. He whinnied when he saw her. Lauren led him towards the far corner of the field. It was shaded by trees and hidden from the house by the stable block.

As soon as they were out of sight of the house, Lauren carefully pulled a single hair out of Twilight's mane, opened the book and took the flower out of her pocket. The gold spots on the petals seemed to glow in the last rays of the sun.

She looked up. The final curve of the sun was just sinking on the horizon. Lauren's eyes narrowed as she searched for the star. But there was nothing. Maybe she had missed it? Twilight whickered.

'Ssh, Twilight,' Lauren said. She turned and patted his neck. Then she looked back up into the sky, and she gasped. High above her, a star had appeared. It was time for the spell!

'Please work,' Lauren whispered. She took a deep, trembling breath and began to tear the petals off the flower. As she did so, she read the spell out.

'Twilight Star, Twilight Star,
Twinkling high above so far.
Shining light, shining bright,
Will you grant my wish tonight?
Let my little horse forlorn
Be at last a unicorn!'

As she read the last word, she held her breath.

Nothing happened.

Lauren looked down at the petals in her hand and felt a

wave of disappointment hit her. It was just a story after all.

She looked at Twilight and felt tears prickle in her eyes. She had so badly wanted him to be a unicorn.

Swallowing hard, she dropped the petals on the ground.

There was a flash of purple light, so bright that it made Lauren shut her eyes. When she opened them again, she gasped.

Twilight had disappeared!

Chapter Nine

Lauren swung around, looking for Twilight. A snow-white unicorn was flying in the sky behind her. Its hooves and horn gleamed silver and its mane and tail swirled around it.

'Twilight?' Lauren gasped.

'Yes,' the unicorn said. 'It's me. It feels a bit wobbly up here. This is the first time I've flown. Whoops . . .' He flew down through the air towards Lauren, narrowly missing a low branch. With a kick of his hind legs, he landed on the grass beside her. 'Hello,' he said, walking over and nuzzling her.

Although Twilight's words rang out clearly in Lauren's head, his mouth didn't move.

'You can talk!' Lauren said in astonishment.

'Only while I'm in my magical shape,' Twilight told her. 'And you'll only be able to hear me if you're touching me or holding a hair from my mane.'

'I can't believe you're really a unicorn!' Lauren exclaimed.

Twilight laughed. 'Well, I am. I was trapped in my pony body, but you freed me, Lauren, and that means you are my Unicorn Friend.'

'Unicorn Friend?' Lauren echoed.

Twilight nodded his beautiful head. 'Yes. Every unicorn is looking for a Unicorn Friend to do good deeds with.'

'So everything in that book is true?' Lauren gasped.

'Everything,' Twilight replied, merrily tossing his mane. He knelt down by bending his forelegs. 'Climb on my back and let's try flying together. You'll have to excuse me if I'm a bit wobbly.'

Lauren took hold of his mane and mounted. 'What if I fall off?'

'You can't fall while I am in my magical shape,' Twilight said. 'Unicorn magic will keep you safe.'

Lauren grabbed his mane and he plunged forward into a canter. 'Whoa . . . hold on tight!' Twilight called.

Twilight's hooves skimmed across the grass and the ground dropped away. 'Here we go!' he called to her.

His back legs kicked down powerfully and with a jolt they flew up into the air, lurching from side to side.

'Don't worry, I'll soon get the hang of this,' Twilight said confidently.

Lauren held on tight. 'Wow!' she gasped as she looked down.

Twilight surged upwards towards the stars and the wind streamed through Lauren's hair as they settled into a steadier pace.

'This is amazing!' she cried.

She looked down. Below her she could see her house and the woods.

Suddenly Lauren caught sight of a figure walking out of the trees. A white terrier dog with a black patch trotted at the person's side. 'It's Mrs Fontana!' she exclaimed.

The old lady looked up and raised her hand in greeting.

'Hello there!' she called.

Twilight swooped towards her and landed lightly on the soft grass.

Lauren scrambled off Twilight's back.

'Mrs Fontana!' she gasped.

Mrs Fontana smiled at Lauren. 'I see you've found yourself a friend.'

Lauren nodded. 'Thank you for giving me the book!' she said.

'It was time it had a new owner,' Mrs Fontana replied. 'But you must promise to guard the secret carefully. A unicorn's powers can attract bad people who want to use the magic selfishly. You must not tell a soul. Do you understand?'

At first Lauren felt disappointed. She had been thinking how amazed her mum and dad would be when she told them. But she could see the sense in what Mrs Fontana was saying. 'I understand,' she said. 'And I promise I won't tell anyone.'

'Good,' Mrs Fontana said. 'Now,' she went on, seeming to produce a piece of paper out of thin air, 'I will give you the Undoing Spell that will turn Twilight back into a pony. Say it when you return home.'

With that, Mrs Fontana handed the paper to Lauren and Lauren read the words:

> 'Twilight Star, Twilight Star,
> Twinkling high above so far,
> Protect this secret from prying eyes
> And return my unicorn to his disguise.
> His magical shape is for my eyes only,
> Let him be once more a pony.'

'Keep Twilight's secret, Lauren,' Mrs Fontana reminded her.

'I will,' Lauren promised.

Twilight bent his knees again and Lauren climbed on to his back.

With two bounds he cantered across the grass and rose up into the sky.

'Bye, Mrs Fontana!' Lauren called, catching hold of his mane.

The old lady raised her hand. 'Use the magic well, my dear,' she called and, with that, she and Walter disappeared into the dark wood.

Twilight and Lauren flew through the sky. Lauren thought she had never felt happier or more excited. There was so much to see. They flew over the woods and rivers, and Mrs Fontana's bookshop, and finally they flew out over the mountains that rose behind Granger's Farm.

At last they returned to the paddock. As they flew down, Lauren suddenly remembered about her parents.

'Twilight!' she gasped. 'I hope Mum and Dad aren't worried about me.'

'Don't worry,' Twilight told her. 'We haven't been gone very long.'

'Oh, Twilight,' Lauren said, 'this is all so exciting!'

Twilight nodded eagerly. 'And the excitement's only just beginning. Soon we'll be having all sorts of adventures together.' He nuzzled her leg. 'I'm so happy you're my Unicorn Friend.'

Lauren hugged him. 'And I'm so happy you're my unicorn.'

As Lauren dismounted, she took the piece of paper that Mrs Fontana had given her out of her pocket. Slowly she read out the Undoing Spell. As she spoke the last word, there was a flash of blinding purple light and suddenly Lauren felt cold air on her face. She opened her eyes. She was still standing beside Twilight, but he was no longer a unicorn; he was just a small grey pony. For a moment Lauren wondered if she'd imagined everything, but then she looked down at the piece of paper in her hand. No, it had been real.

'Goodnight,' Lauren whispered, kissing him in delight. Then, picking up the book from the grass, she turned and ran to the house.

As she hurried in, Buddy bounded over to greet her, almost knocking her down in his excitement.

Her dad was washing up the supper dishes at the sink and her mum was pouring Max a drink.

'How was Twilight?' her mum asked.

'He was fine,' Lauren said. 'I . . . I think I might just go up to my room and read for a while.'

She went upstairs and sat down by her bedroom window. Twilight was grazing in his paddock. Seeming to sense that Lauren was looking at him, he raised his head and whinnied.

A broad grin crept across Lauren's face.

Her new pony had turned out to be her secret unicorn.

What adventures they were going to have!

Lauren's Factfile

AGE: Nine

HEIGHT: 130 cm

HAIR COLOUR:
Long, slightly wavy fair hair

EYES: Green

BEST FRIENDS:
Mel Cassidy, Jessica Parker,
Carly and Anna in the city,
and of course, Twilight!

FAVOURITE FOOD:
Pasta

FAVOURITE TREAT:
Home-made cookies

FAVOURITE BOOK:
The Life of a Unicorn
and Black Beauty

LIKES:
Ponies, sleepovers, reading books,
riding camp and – best of all – flying with Twilight!

DISLIKES:
People who neglect their animals
and rainy days

HOBBIES:
Horse-riding, gymkhanas, painting
and drawing, writing stories

FAVOURITE POEM:
'The Turning Spell'

Twilight Star, Twilight Star,
Twinkling high above so far.
Shining light, shining bright,
Will you grant my wish tonight?
Let my little horse forlorn
Be at last a unicorn!

Twilight's Factfile

AGE: Seven

HEIGHT: Thirteen hands

COLOUR: Grey

EYES: Chestnut brown

BEST PONY PAL:
Shadow (Mel's pony)

FAVOURITE FOOD:
Oats

FAVOURITE TREAT:
Carrots!

BEST FRIEND:
Lauren!

BEST FRIEND:
Buddy, Max's
Bernese mountain dog puppy

LIKES:
Flying with Lauren and discovering
new unicorn powers. Going out on rides
and having picnics by the creek

DISLIKES:
Bad manners and people who
aren't nice to their ponies

FAVOURITE PONY ACTIVITY:
Trekking with Lauren or
paddling in the creek

FAVOURITE UNICORN ACTIVITY:
Healing and helping animals and
people with special
magical powers

Dreams Come True

Chapter One

'It's almost time, Twilight,' Lauren Foster whispered to the grey pony beside her. She looked down at the star-shaped flower in her hand. This was the moment she'd been waiting for all day. As the last of the sun disappeared behind the mountains, a bright star shone out overhead.

A thrill ran through Lauren. *Now!*

Gently, she began to crumble the petals between her fingers. As she did so, she whispered the secret words of the Turning Spell.

'Twilight Star, Twilight Star,
Twinkling high above so far.
Shining light, shining bright,
Will you grant my wish tonight?
Let my little horse forlorn
Be at last a unicorn!'

Almost before the last word had left Lauren's mouth, there was a bright purple flash.

The patch of grass where Twilight had been standing was empty. Lauren looked up. A snow-white unicorn was cantering in circles in the sky.

'Twilight!' Lauren exclaimed in delight.

Twilight swooped down and landed beside Lauren.

'Hello,' he said, putting his nose close to hers and blowing out softly. Although Twilight's words rang out clearly in Lauren's head, his mouth didn't move. As long as she was touching him, or holding a hair from his mane, she would be able to hear him speaking.

Lauren hugged him and then looked down at the petals still

clutched in her hand. 'But I didn't throw them on the ground,' she said.

Twilight tossed his flowing silver mane. 'You don't need to any more. The moonflower petals are only needed the *first* time the spell is said. You don't even need the light of the Twilight Star. From now on, all you need to do is say the magic words.' He pawed the grass. 'Come on, Lauren. Let's go flying.'

Twilight plunged upwards and Lauren laughed in delight as the wind whipped through her hair. She held on to Twilight's long mane.

'Let's fly over the woods,' Twilight said. 'And jump over the treetops.'

Twilight turned in the air and headed for the forest that covered the mountains behind Lauren's house.

Lauren could see the nearby farms spread out beneath them. One in particular caught her attention – a white clapboard farmhouse with red barns that hugged the mountainside at the edge of the forest. 'That's Goose Creek Farm,' she said. 'Dad met the man who owns it today. He's called Mr Cassidy. He's got a daughter called Mel who's the same age as me and she's got a pony. Dad's arranged for me to go and visit them tomorrow and you're coming too!'

'Sounds like fun!' Twilight said.

Lauren suddenly looked anxious.

'What if Mel's pony guesses you're a unicorn?' she said. She knew that it was very important no one discovered Twilight's secret. Lauren had been given the spell to turn Twilight into a unicorn by an old lady called Mrs Fontana, and she had told Lauren that she must never let anyone find out Twilight was a unicorn. It might put him in great danger!

'He'll know,' Twilight said, 'but it'll be OK. Horses and ponies understand that a unicorn's secret must be kept.'

'Do all animals know about unicorns?' Lauren asked curiously.

Twilight shook his head. 'Just horses and ponies, though sometimes other animals will sense I'm different.' He swooped down so that his hooves were skimming the treetops. 'Now, are you ready to do some jumping?'

'You bet!' Lauren exclaimed.

They leapt from one treetop to the next, giddy with excitement.

All too soon, Lauren realized it was time to go back home. 'If we're much longer, Mum and Dad might start getting worried,' she said to Twilight.

He nodded and they flew back to Granger's Farm.

Twilight landed in his paddock. Lauren dismounted and said the Undoing Spell. There was a bright purple flash as Twilight turned from a unicorn into a small grey pony.

'See you tomorrow,' Lauren whispered. She gave him a quick hug, then raced back to the house.

Her dad was in the kitchen. He glanced at the kitchen clock.

'You've been out a long time,' he commented.

'I was just playing with Twilight,' Lauren said, her heart pounding.

To her relief, her dad smiled. 'I'm glad you're enjoying having a pony so much,' he said. 'Life here in the country sure beats life back in the city, doesn't it?'

'Totally,' Lauren agreed happily.

As Lauren passed her brother's bedroom, she heard laughter. She pushed the door open. Her brother, Max, was in bed and Buddy, Max's Bernese mountain dog puppy, was standing on his hind legs with his big white front paws on the covers. His pink tongue was hanging out and he seemed to be trying to lick every inch of Max's face.

Buddy came gambolling over to Lauren. Not managing to stop in time, he skidded into her legs.

'Oof!' Lauren exclaimed. 'Buddy! You weigh a ton!'

'You wait till he's fully grown,' Mum said with a laugh. 'Now you'd better get ready for bed too, honey. You and Dad are expected at the Cassidys' house at nine-thirty so you're going to have to get up early to get Twilight fed and groomed in time.'

Lauren nodded.

As she went to her bedroom, she thought about the next day. Would Mel want to be friends with her? Would she want to be friends with Mel? She hoped so.

She went over to her bedroom window. She could see the Blue Ridge Mountains towering up behind the house and, best of all, she could see Twilight's stable and paddock.

'Goodnight, Twilight,' she whispered, looking at the little pony's shadowy shape grazing by the gate.

Twilight looked up. Lauren was sure she saw him whicker. Blowing him a kiss, she smiled and closed the curtain.

Chapter Two

Lauren got up early the next morning to get Twilight ready. The April sun was shining as she stepped outside and the new leaves on the trees looked green and fresh. She ran down the path that led from the house to the paddock. Twilight was waiting at the gate. He whinnied when he saw her.

'Hi, fella,' Lauren said, climbing over the gate. 'I bet you'd like some breakfast.'

Twilight nuzzled her. Snapping the leadrope on to his head-collar, Lauren led him up to his stable and fetched him some pony nuts in a bucket. As he ate, she looked at her watch. Eight-fifteen. That meant she had an hour to groom him before she and her dad had to leave for the Cassidys' house.

Half an hour later, Lauren stepped back to admire her handiwork. Twilight's scruffy grey coat was looking much cleaner, his hooves gleamed from the hoof oil and his newly washed tail was almost dry.

'You look loads better,' Lauren declared. He whickered in agreement.

'Buddy! Come back!'

Hearing her brother's cry, Lauren looked round. Buddy was galloping down the path towards her, his enormous white paws thudding on the grass. Max tore after him.

'Buddy! Careful!' Lauren gasped, as the puppy headed straight for the bucket of water. Buddy crashed into it, sending the dirty suds flying up into the air.

Twilight snorted and jumped back to the end of his rope, but the contents of the bucket splashed all over him.

'Buddy!' Lauren exclaimed. She swung round to Max.

He was standing on the path, his blue eyes wide with shock. 'Max!' she cried.

'I'm sorry,' Max said. 'I opened the back door and Buddy just ran out. I couldn't stop him, Lauren.'

Lauren sighed. It was no use getting annoyed with Max. It wasn't his fault that Buddy was so clumsy. 'It's OK,' she said. 'I guess I'll just have to groom Twilight again.'

'Look at Buddy,' Max said suddenly.

Lauren looked at the puppy. He was crawling on his tummy towards Twilight, his ears pricked up, his tail wagging like crazy. 'Woof!' he said, jumping back.

'What's he doing?' Max said in surprise.

'I don't know,' Lauren said with a frown. She felt worried. Could Buddy somehow sense that Twilight wasn't a normal pony? She got hold of Buddy's collar. 'Here, Max. Maybe you should take him back to the house. Twilight might stand on him by mistake if he gets too close.'

As Max dragged Buddy back to the house, Lauren bit her lip. If Buddy acted like that in front of her mum and dad, they were bound to get suspicious. She looked at Twilight. He was staring after Buddy, and Lauren was sure he looked concerned.

At nine-fifteen, Lauren rode out of Granger's Farm with her father walking beside Twilight. They headed for Goose Creek Farm. It wasn't far and they were soon walking down the drive towards the house. The back door opened and a tall man with black hair came out to greet them.

'Mike!' he said, shaking Mr Foster's hand. 'Hi. And this must be Lauren. Mel can't wait to meet you. She's with Shadow – that's her pony. Come on, I'll show you round to the paddock.'

Lauren rode after him. As they reached the back of the house, she saw a paddock with two jumps set out. A dapple-grey pony was tethered to the paddock fence. A girl with black curly hair was standing beside him, brushing his shiny coat.

'Mel!' Mr Cassidy called.

The girl turned. Seeing Lauren, her face lit up with a friendly grin. 'Hi!' she called. Throwing her grooming brush down, she jogged over. 'I'm Mel.'

'I'm Lauren,' Lauren said rather shyly.

'Your pony's gorgeous,' Mel said. 'What's he called?'

'Twilight,' said Lauren, dismounting.

'Twilight,' Mel frowned thoughtfully, patting him. 'Did he used to belong to Jade Roberts?'

'That's right,' Lauren said in surprise.

Mel nodded. 'I thought I recognized him. I go to Pony Club with Jade.' She smiled at Lauren. 'My pony's called Shadow. Do you want to come and meet him?'

Lauren nodded eagerly.

'We'll leave you two girls to get to know each other then,' Mr Cassidy said. 'We'll be in the house if you want us.'

Lauren and Mel nodded. 'So, how long have you had Shadow?' Lauren asked, as she led Twilight over to say hello.

'Six months,' Mel replied. 'I'd wanted a pony for . . . like forever. I think I was born pony-crazy.'

'Me too!' Lauren agreed, grinning at her.

Shadow turned his head to look at Twilight. Lauren held her breath. What if he acted as strangely as Buddy had?

But, after staring at Twilight for a moment, Shadow simply snorted softly and stretched out his muzzle to say hello.

Twilight blew down his nostrils in reply.

'They like each other!' Mel said. She beamed at Lauren. 'It's going to be so cool being neighbours – I can just tell!'

Lauren and Mel had great fun. Shadow was fast and could turn very quickly, but Twilight was also pretty speedy. They chased each other round and round, had an egg-and-spoon race, a trotting race and a race where they had to canter around poles stuck in the ground in a line. 'This is loads better than riding on my own!' Mel said, as they finished in a dead heat.

'Shall we jump next?' Lauren asked, looking at the fences.

Mel's face fell. 'There's no point,' she sighed. 'Shadow doesn't jump. I took him to a Pony Club mounted meeting last month but he wouldn't even go near a jump. Watch.'

She cantered Shadow away from Twilight and turned him towards one of the fences. He slowed to a trot and then to a walk. He stopped a metre away from the jump.

'He does it every time,' Mel said, riding back to Lauren. 'And I don't know what I'm going to do. There's another mounted meeting this Saturday and Jade Roberts and her friend Monica were really mean about him when he wouldn't jump last time.'

Although Mel tried to smile, Lauren could see the sadness in her new friend's eyes. 'I'll try to think of some way to help,' she promised. 'If I come over tomorrow after school, maybe we could try again then.'

'That would be great,' Mel said, looking more cheerful. 'Between the two of us we must be able to think of something.'

They untacked the ponies and turned them out into the paddock to graze. Then Mel showed Lauren around the farm. Just up the track from the barn with Shadow's stall was an enormous red hay-barn. In it was Mel's cat, Sparkle. 'She's just had two kittens,' Mel said to Lauren.

Lauren gasped in delight as she saw the two tiny black kittens snuggled into their mother's side. Sparkle had made a nest in a pile of loose hay at the back of the barn and the two kittens were sleeping beside her.

'What have you called them?' Lauren asked in a low voice.

'Star and Midnight,' Mel whispered back.

As they walked back down the path towards the paddock and the farmhouse, Mel turned to Lauren. 'You should join Pony Club too. We have mounted and unmounted meetings every month, competitions, and there's even a camp in the summer!'

Lauren hesitated, thinking about the two girls who had been mean to Mel.

Mel seemed to read her mind. 'It's only Jade and Monica who are like that,' she said. 'The others in my group are really nice.'

'OK then,' Lauren agreed. 'I'll ask.'

'You two look like you've been having fun,' Mr Foster said, as Lauren and Mel ran into the large kitchen.

'We have!' Lauren exclaimed. 'We went riding and then Mel showed me round, and she wants to know if I can join her Pony Club.'

She looked at Mel, who nodded eagerly.

Mr Foster smiled. 'It sounds like a great idea.'

'It's a good Pony Club,' said Mr Cassidy. 'There's a mounted meeting next weekend. Lauren and Twilight are very welcome to have a ride there in our trailer.'

'Thanks,' said Mr Foster.

Lauren and Mel exchanged delighted looks.

'I'm so glad you've moved here,' Mel said, as Lauren got back on Twilight to ride home.

'Me too,' Lauren said, grinning at her.

'I'll see you at school tomorrow,' Mel called.

'So, do you like Mel, then?' Mr Foster said to Lauren, as they walked along the road.

'Yeah!' Lauren said. 'She's lots of fun.' She stroked Twilight's neck. She couldn't stop thinking about Shadow's jumping problem. She really wanted to help. But how?

Maybe Twilight will know, she thought.

Chapter Three

After supper, Lauren pulled on her trainers. The sun had just set and she was anxious to get moving. 'I'm just going to check on Twilight,' she said to her mum.

'OK, honey,' Mrs Foster said. 'But don't be out for too long. Remember you've got school starting tomorrow.'

Buddy ran to the door and stood there, his head cocked on one side.

'You're not coming with me, Buddy,' Lauren told him. She went outside, shutting the door carefully behind her, and hurried down the path to the paddock. Would Twilight be able to think of a way to help Shadow?

Twilight whickered when he saw her. Lauren had just begun to say the words of the Turning Spell when suddenly Twilight whinnied loudly.

Buddy was standing on the path behind her.

'Buddy! Go away!' Lauren exclaimed.

'Buddy!' she heard her dad shouting.

'He's here, Dad!' Lauren called back.

Mr Foster came down the path. 'I only opened the door for a second. Buddy just raced off after you. Come on, fella,' he said, taking hold of the puppy's collar. 'You come in with me.'

Lauren waited until she heard the door of the house shut and then whispered the secret words.

There was a purple flash and suddenly Twilight was standing before her, a snow-white unicorn once again.

'That was close,' he said.

'I'm going to have to be so careful,' Lauren said, 'Buddy's far too interested in you.' Suddenly she remembered what she'd been going to ask Twilight. 'Do you know why Shadow won't jump? Mel's really upset about it.'

'I don't know,' Twilight admitted. 'But we could visit him later and find out.'

'All right,' Lauren agreed. 'I'll come back as soon as I can.' She said the Undoing Spell, turning Twilight back into a pony, and hurried back to the house.

After her mum had said goodnight and gone into her study to work, Lauren pulled her jeans on over her pyjamas and crept down the stairs and out of the house.

I'll be back as quickly as I can, she told herself as she hurried down to the paddock.

It only took a few seconds to change Twilight into a unicorn. 'Quick!' Lauren said. She scrambled on to his back. 'Let's go!'

They swooped down on Shadow's paddock at Goose Creek Farm. 'There he is!' Lauren said.

Twilight landed with a soft whicker just behind him. Shadow swung round with an alarmed snort.

Twilight whinnied and Lauren saw Shadow relax.

Lauren didn't want to waste any time. 'Ask him why he won't jump,' she said to Twilight.

'He understands you,' Twilight told her as Shadow whinnied in reply. Twilight listened to the dapple-grey pony for a few moments. 'He's scared,' he told Lauren. 'He says that when he was a foal, he was jumping over a tree trunk and he banged his legs really hard. Ever since then, he's been afraid of jumping. He hates making Mel upset but he just can't do it.'

'Have you got any magical powers that could help him not to feel so scared, Twilight?' Lauren asked.

'I don't know,' Twilight replied doubtfully. 'I know I've got some magical powers, but I'm not sure what they are.'

Lauren felt disappointed. She'd been hoping that Twilight would be able to do some magic and make everything OK. She thought hard. If they couldn't use Twilight's powers to help Shadow then maybe she could come up with a more practical solution.

She got off Twilight's back and took two poles from the jumps and laid them out on the grass.

'Try walking over these,' she said to Shadow. 'At least it's a step towards jumping.'

Shadow walked up to the first pole and stopped. Then, snorting loudly, he stepped over it, picking his hooves up high.

'Well done!' Lauren cried. 'Now try the other one, Shadow.'

The same thing happened.

'You did it!' Twilight exclaimed.

'I'll put up a tiny jump now,' Lauren said. 'Let's see if you can do that.'

But Shadow backed off, whinnying.

Twilight sighed. 'He doesn't want to. He's still too frightened. If we can come and help him some more, he might get braver.'

'OK, we'll come again tomorrow,' Lauren said. 'We'll help you, Shadow. No matter how long it takes.'

Chapter Four

'Come on, Lauren!' Mrs Foster called the next morning. Lauren checked her reflection for the last time in her bedroom mirror. She was wearing new jeans and a blue T-shirt. Her freshly washed hair was tied back in a ponytail. She swallowed nervously. Her first day at a new school. What was it going to be like?

Silver River Elementary School was only a ten-minute drive away from Granger's Farm. As Mrs Foster parked the car, Lauren saw Mel standing at the school gates. 'There's Mel!' she exclaimed.

She jumped out of the car and ran over. 'Hi!'

'Hi!' Mel said. 'I thought I'd wait for you.'

Mrs Foster and Max walked up to them. 'This is my mum and my brother, Max,' Lauren said.

'Pleased to meet you,' Mel said politely. 'I'm in the same class as Lauren, Mrs Foster. I can show her there if you want.'

Mrs Foster looked questioningly at Lauren, who nodded. 'I'll be fine, Mum,' she said quickly.

'Well, that would be a real help, Mel. It gives me more time to get Max settled into his classroom. I'll stop by the office, Lauren, and tell them you're here.'

'Bye, Mum,' said Lauren, giving her a quick kiss.

'Have a good day, honey.'

'She will,' Mel said. 'Come on, Lauren. I want to show you round.'

By morning break, Lauren's nerves had totally disappeared. Mr Noland, her new teacher, was strict but fun. Even better, he'd let her and Mel sit together. The other kids in the class seemed really keen to be friends too – all apart from Jade Roberts and her friend Monica Corder. They hadn't said a word to Lauren or Mel, although they had giggled when Jade had leaned over Mel's desk and caught sight of a horse that Mel had drawn.

'Looks more like a pig than a horse,' Jade had said to Monica. 'Just like her dumb pony. I mean, imagine having a dumb pony that won't jump. How sad can you get?'

'He's not dumb!' Lauren said angrily.

Jade turned her full attention to her. 'And what do *you* know about horses?'

'Well, I've got one,' Lauren said.

'Lauren Foster?' Jade said suddenly. 'You're the girl who owns Twilight, aren't you?' When Lauren nodded, Jade laughed. 'How sad. I got my dad to sell him because he wasn't good enough to win ribbons. My new pony, Prince, is a hundred times better.'

Lauren glared at them but, before she could say anything, Mr Noland heard the whispering and told Jade and Monica to be quiet.

Lauren was still fuming when the lesson came to an end.

'Come on, Lauren!' Mel said as they went outside. 'Let's go and sit under the tree. I've brought some photos of Shadow to show you.'

'You know I had an idea last night,' Lauren said quickly, wanting to cheer her up. 'I think Shadow might be scared of jumping . . . for some reason. We could try walking him over poles on the ground, then, as he gets braver, we could put up some tiny jumps.'

Mel looked doubtful. 'Do you really think it will work?'

'I'm sure,' Lauren said. 'Look, why don't I come over after school with Twilight and we can try then?'

Her enthusiasm seemed to encourage Mel.

'OK,' she said eagerly. 'Let's do it.'

Chapter Five

'Should I try now?' Mel said to Lauren later that afternoon. She was mounted on Shadow and nervously looking at the poles that she and Lauren had laid out on the grass.

'Yes,' Lauren said, patting Twilight. 'Just trot him over them.'

Mel turned Shadow towards the poles. The little dapple-grey pony glanced once at Twilight, and then trotted bravely over them.

'He did it!' Mel exclaimed in astonishment.

By the time Shadow had trotted over the poles ten times, Mel was beaming from ear to ear. 'Maybe I'll be able to get him to jump after all,' she said.

After untacking the ponies and turning them out into Shadow's paddock to graze, Lauren and Mel went up the path to see Sparkle and her two kittens in the barn.

Star and Midnight were awake.

'Which one's which?' Lauren asked. They looked identical to her.

'Star's got a white star shape on her tummy,' Mel explained. She picked up the kitten nearest her. 'Look.'

'Oh, yes!' Lauren laughed, seeing the white hairs.

'Do you want to hold her?' Mel asked.

Lauren nodded eagerly and Mel handed Star over.

'Hello,' Lauren murmured. 'Aren't you lovely?' Star cuddled into her arms.

'Wasn't Shadow good today?' Mel said. 'I just wish he could learn to jump in time for the meeting on Saturday. Jade and Monica are being so mean about him.' She looked at Lauren hopefully. 'Do you think we might have him jumping soon?'

'We might,' Lauren said. 'Fingers crossed.'

As Lauren rode Twilight home, she couldn't stop thinking about Mel's words.

If only we could teach Shadow to jump more quickly, she thought.

She remembered what Twilight had said about his powers – he had some but he didn't know what they were. Maybe he did have some magic that could help. But how could they find out?

And then the answer came to her. *Mrs Fontana*. Mrs Fontana was the only other person in the world who knew Twilight's secret. She'd given Lauren an old book that contained the words of the Turning Spell. If anyone would be able to help, she would.

As soon as she got home, Lauren ran into the house. Her mum was working on her computer.

'Mum,' Lauren said, 'can you take me to Mrs Fontana's bookshop?'

Mrs Foster frowned. 'Why?'

Lauren didn't know what to say. 'I . . . I want to ask her something . . . about a project I'm doing. I thought she might be able to help.'

'Well, actually, I was going to go into town,' Mrs Foster said. 'I need to get some film for the camera. You could go and see Mrs Fontana while I pick up the film.'

'Great!' Lauren said.

Almost before Mrs Foster had parked, Lauren scrambled out of the car. She raced over to the bookshop. A chime jangled as she pushed open the door.

Walter, Mrs Fontana's terrier, came trotting over.

'Hi, boy,' Lauren said, bending down to pat him. As she straightened up, she saw that the old lady had appeared, as if by magic. Mrs Fontana's face was lined and wrinkled but her blue eyes shone out, bright and clear.

'Hello, Lauren,' she said. 'What can I do for you today?'

Lauren hesitated. 'Well . . . er . . .'

Mrs Fontana looked over her shoulder to where a couple of people were browsing along a bookshelf. 'Come down to the children's section,' she said softly.

Lauren followed Mrs Fontana. There was an armchair and cushions on the floor. 'So how's Twilight?' Mrs Fontana said, sitting down.

'Fine,' Lauren replied. She lowered her voice. 'We're trying to help this pony, Mrs Fontana. He belongs to my friend and he's scared of jumping.' She quickly explained about Shadow. 'He's so scared that it might take ages to get him jumping properly,' she said. 'Do you know if Twilight has any magical powers that could help?'

Mrs Fontana smiled. 'Twilight has many magical powers, Lauren. But I cannot tell you what they are. A unicorn has to discover his powers for himself.' She leaned forward and took Lauren's hands in hers. 'Don't worry, Twilight is able to help this pony,' she said. 'But it is up to you to help him work out how, Lauren. You became a Unicorn Friend because you have a good heart and the imagination to believe in magic. Use those qualities and together you and Twilight will discover his powers.'

Mrs Fontana got to her feet. She smiled at Lauren. 'Good luck with Shadow, Lauren. I hope you and Twilight can find a way to help.'

With that, Mrs Fontana went to the front of the shop where someone was waiting to pay for their books.

The shop door opened and Mrs Foster walked in. Lauren ran over. 'Hi, Mum.'

'Are you ready to go?' Mrs Foster asked.

Lauren nodded. 'Bye, Mrs Fontana,' she said, glancing over to the desk where the old woman was wrapping up the customer's purchases.

Mrs Fontana looked up. 'Goodbye, Lauren,' she said. She smiled. 'And good luck.'

Chapter Six

That evening, Lauren crept out of the house again. 'Let's be quick,' she said, getting on to Twilight's back.

As they flew to Goose Creek Farm, she told him what Mrs Fontana had said. 'You have got powers that can help Shadow,' she told him.

'But how can I use them if I don't know what they are?' Twilight said.

'I don't know,' Lauren admitted.

Shadow was waiting for them. He whinnied.

'You were great today, Shadow!' Twilight said as he landed.

Shadow bowed his head, as if a bit embarrassed by the praise.

'What about trying a small jump?' Lauren suggested hopefully.

Shadow hesitated for a moment and then slowly nodded his head.

Before Shadow could change his mind, Lauren scrambled off Twilight and put up a tiny jump. 'You can do it, Shadow!' she said.

Shadow nodded his head and, turning towards the hump, he began to trot.

'He's going to do it!' Lauren gasped to Twilight.

But then Shadow stopped dead.

'Oh dear,' Lauren sighed.

She and Twilight trotted over.

'What went wrong?' Lauren asked him. 'Why did you stop?'

The dapple-grey pony hung his head and snorted sadly.

'He was just too scared,' Twilight told Lauren.

Twilight stepped forward and touched his glowing horn to Shadow's neck. 'It's OK,' Lauren heard him say softly. 'You tried your best. Don't be upset.'

They stood there for a moment, and then Lauren saw the little dapple-grey pony's ears flicker forward. He raised his head and whickered in a surprised sort of way.

'What's he saying?' Lauren asked Twilight.

'That he's feeling a bit better,' Twilight replied.

Shadow whickered again.

'Much better,' Twilight said.

Lauren saw Shadow look at the jump. His eyes suddenly seemed to be full of confidence.

'In fact, he says he feels so much better that he thinks he might be able to clear the jump,' Twilight said, looking astonished.

Shadow pricked up his ears and trotted away from them. Turning towards the jump, he started to canter. Lauren and Twilight watched in amazement as he flew over it.

'He jumped it!' Lauren exclaimed.

Shadow came cantering back to them, whinnying.

'He says that when we were talking he suddenly felt really brave,' Twilight said.

Shadow nuzzled Twilight and suddenly Lauren's eyes widened. 'Your horn!' she exclaimed to Twilight. 'You were touching him with your horn when he started to feel brave. Perhaps that's one of your magical powers. Maybe by touching him you gave him your courage – a unicorn's bravery.'

Shadow nodded his head, and then he turned and cantered over the jump again.

Lauren hugged Twilight in delight. 'This is brilliant!' she said. 'Mel is going to be so pleased.'

★

Lauren was even more pleased by their night's work when Jade started teasing Mel again the next day at lunchtime.

'Still going to the meeting on Saturday, Mel?' Jade asked, coming over to them as they put their trays away. 'I don't know why you're bothering. It's not like Shadow will jump. Can't your parents afford to buy you a better pony?'

'Mel doesn't want another pony,' Lauren said, unable to bear their teasing a second longer. 'Shadow's fine.'

Jade laughed. 'Yeah, right,' she said, walking off laughing.

Lauren looked at her friend. Mel was biting her lip in frustration. 'I hate her!' she burst out. 'I think I'm just going to tell Dad that I don't want to go on Saturday.'

'You can't,' Lauren said. 'You've got to come, Mel. If you don't Jade and Monica will tease you again next week. Shadow will be good. In fact, I'm sure he's going to jump.'

Mel looked at her doubtfully. 'You think so?'

'I know so,' Lauren said confidently.

As soon as Lauren got home after school, she rode Twilight round to Mel's. 'I can't wait to see her face when Shadow jumps,' Lauren said to him, as they trotted along the road.

Mel was just putting Shadow's saddle on when they arrived. When they rode into the paddock, Lauren set up the jump exactly as she had done the night before. Then she got back on Twilight. 'Try Shadow now!' she called to Mel.

'OK,' Mel said. She turned Shadow towards the jump. His ears pricked up and he quickened his stride.

'He's going to jump it!' Lauren whispered to Twilight in delight.

Shadow got nearer and nearer, his hooves thudding on the grass.

Then, a metre in front of the jump, he suddenly stopped.

Chapter Seven

Lauren gasped in disappointment.

Twilight snorted and Lauren knew he was just as surprised as she was that Shadow had stopped.

Mel rode back to Lauren looking bitterly disappointed. 'I guess I should have known better than to think he would jump it,' she said. Shadow hung his head sadly. Mel hugged him. 'Don't worry, boy. I still love you.'

'I'm sorry, Mel,' Lauren said, as they dismounted.

'It's not your fault,' Mel said with a sigh.

Lauren had a feeling that Mel wanted to be on her own and so, after a bit, she got back on to Twilight and rode him home.

'What went wrong?' she said to him.

Twilight shook his head and snorted.

'I'll come down to your paddock tonight,' Lauren told him. 'We've got to sort this out.'

She was grooming Twilight back at Granger's Farm when Buddy came running down the path towards them. He skidded to a stop, sat down and, cocking his head on one side, whined at Twilight.

Just then, Max came running down the path. 'There you are, Buddy!' he said, as the puppy trotted over to meet him. Buddy licked his hand and then turned back to Twilight and woofed.

Max frowned. 'Why does Buddy act so weird around Twilight, Lauren?'

'I don't know,' Lauren said. 'Look, I'm trying to groom him. Why don't you take Buddy for a walk, Max?'

But Max didn't seem to be listening. 'Maybe Twilight's an alien, Lauren!' he gasped.

'An alien?' Lauren stared at him.

'Yeah, maybe Twilight's an alien from another planet. He's in disguise so that he can spy on us and Buddy knows it.'

'Don't be dumb, Twilight's just a pony,' Lauren said, desperately trying to act as if Max was totally crazy.

But Max didn't look convinced. 'I'm going to tell Mum and Dad,' he said, running back up the path.

Lauren was sure her mum would just laugh at Max's idea about aliens, but the last thing she wanted was Max going on and on saying that there was something odd about Twilight.

'See all the trouble you're causing?' she said to Buddy, who was sniffing at Twilight's tail.

Chapter Eight

It was Lauren's turn to help wash the dishes after supper. Once they were all dried and put away, she pulled on her boots. 'I'm going to see Twilight, Mum,' she said.

'OK,' Mrs Foster said. She looked round. 'Anyone seen Max?'

Lauren and her dad shook their heads.

'He's probably in his room drawing Twilight's spaceship,' Mr Foster said with a laugh.

Lauren let herself out of the back door, feeling very relieved that her mum and dad were treating her brother's suspicions as a joke.

'Hi, boy,' she called, as Twilight whinnied to her from the paddock gate. 'Let's go and see Shadow and find out why he wouldn't jump today.'

They flew to Shadow's field. The little dapple-grey pony was standing quietly, still looking very unhappy. He whinnied.

Twilight turned to Lauren. 'Poor Shadow. He says he really wanted to jump today, but he just didn't feel brave enough without the touch of my horn.'

Shadow neighed sadly.

Lauren didn't like to see Shadow looking so upset. 'I don't know what to do,' she told Shadow. 'You know Twilight can't be a unicorn when there are other people around.'

Shadow nodded.

He didn't try jumping again that evening. After all, they knew he *could* jump at night when Twilight was a unicorn – it was jumping in the day that was the problem.

Lauren sighed unhappily as she and Twilight flew home. She really wished there was something they could do to help.

★

The next morning at school, Mel looked serious. 'I've decided that I'm not going to try and jump Shadow ever again,' she told Lauren. 'It just makes him miserable and I'd rather get teased than make him unhappy. I'll just have to put up with whatever Jade and Monica say.'

Lauren squeezed her arm comfortingly.

'Will you still come over with Twilight this afternoon though?' Mel asked. 'We could go for a trail ride.'

Lauren nodded. 'Sure,' she said.

When Lauren got to Goose Creek Farm that afternoon, Mel was already mounted on Shadow. 'We'd better get going,' Mel said. 'Mum thinks there might be a storm coming.'

Lauren looked up at the overcast sky. The air certainly had a heavy, stormy feel about it. They urged Shadow and Twilight into a trot.

Mr Cassidy was fixing a fence near to the hay-barn. 'Don't go out too far,' he called.

'Let's just go into the woods,' Mel said. 'There's a great trail with a sandy bit where we can have a canter.'

A few minutes later, they entered the woods. The trail stretched out in front of them, straight and inviting.

'Are you ready?' Mel asked.

Lauren nodded.

Mel leaned forward and gave Shadow his head. The dapple-grey pony bounded into a canter. Twilight hesitated for a moment and then, when Lauren squeezed his side, he followed.

The wind whipped against Lauren's face as she leaned forward and urged Twilight on. His hooves thudded down on the sand and she could feel a broad grin stretch across her face. This was as good as flying!

At last, the trail began to narrow and they slowed Twilight and

Shadow to a trot and then to a walk.

Suddenly they heard a deep, low rumbling noise. The leaves on the branches nearest to them seemed to shiver slightly.

'Thunder!' Mel said, looking at Lauren in alarm. 'We'd better turn around.'

Shadow and Twilight began to canter along the path. Lauren felt worried. Her parents had warned her lots of times about not being out in a thunderstorm.

As they reached the entrance to the woods, Lauren reined Twilight in. A jagged flash of lightning forked down, lighting up the darkened sky.

'Maybe we should stay here,' Mel stammered, looking frightened.

'No, it's really dangerous to stay near trees,' Lauren said. 'The lightning might strike one of them.' She looked down the path towards the house. 'If we gallop, we'll be back in a minute,' she said, looking at the lights shining invitingly out of the farmhouse's windows. 'Come on!'

They galloped down the track, passing the hay-barn and heading towards the barn with Shadow's stall.

Suddenly, Lauren saw Mel's dad standing in the barn's entrance.

'Quick!' Mr Cassidy shouted. 'Get into the barn!'

Lauren and Mel flung themselves off Twilight and Shadow's backs and ran with them inside.

Suddenly, the sky outside lit up with a bright white flash of lightning. There was a loud bang nearby.

Mr Cassidy ran to the entrance and looked out. 'A tree by the hay-barn's been hit. It's on fire!' he exclaimed. 'I'm going to have to call the fire department. You stay here while I go to the house. I don't want you outside in this.'

'But what about the fire?' Mel cried.

'It's all right. It won't reach you here,' Mr Cassidy said. 'I'll be back as soon as I can.' And with that, he ducked his head and ran out.

Lauren led Twilight to the entrance and looked up the track towards the hay-barn. The tall oak tree that stood next to it was burning brightly.

Mel joined her. 'If it falls, the whole barn will go up in flames! Dad had better be . . .' She broke off, her eyes widening. 'Sparkle!' she cried in horror. 'Lauren, Sparkle and her kittens are inside!'

Chapter Nine

Mel put her foot in the stirrup and swung herself up on to Shadow's back. 'I've got to save Sparkle,' she said, digging her heels into Shadow's sides and heading out.

'It's too dangerous, Mel!' Lauren cried.

But it was too late. Mel was already cantering Shadow up the track towards the barn.

Lauren didn't hesitate. Swinging herself up on Twilight's back, she galloped after her friend. 'Mel! Stop!' she yelled. She hated the thought of Sparkle and the kittens being trapped in the barn, but she knew Mel's life could be in danger if she went inside.

But Mel didn't listen. She urged Shadow past the burning tree and up to the barn door. Jumping off his back, she hauled it open.

Sparkle came racing out. She was carrying one of the kittens in her mouth. Lauren saw a flash of white on the kitten's tummy. Star! But what about Midnight? He must still be inside.

To her horror, Lauren saw Mel loop Shadow's reins over her arm and run into the barn.

Twilight gave an alarmed whinny. There was a loud creak. Lauren looked up. A huge burning branch of the oak tree looked as if it was about to break off.

'Mel!' she shouted. 'Get out!'

Mel appeared on foot in the doorway of the barn, clutching Midnight.

'Quick!' Lauren yelled, looking up at the tree.

But it was too late. Before Mel could get out of the barn, there was a loud crack and the burning branch crashed to the ground in front of the barn door.

Mel screamed and Lauren gasped. The branch was blocking

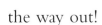

the way out!

There was only one way for Mel to get out.

'Get up on Shadow and make him jump the branch, Mel!' Lauren cried. 'It's the only way.'

'But he won't do it!' Mel shouted.

'Just try!' Lauren called.

Clutching Midnight to her chest, Mel scrambled on to Shadow's back.

Lauren glanced around, desperately hoping to see Mr Cassidy or the fire department arriving, but there was no one there.

She heard Shadow neigh uncertainly through the smoke. *Please jump it*, Lauren prayed. '*You might not have Twilight's magical powers to help you, but you can still do it. Please, Shadow, please!*'

She saw Shadow hesitate and dread gripped her heart.

'Melanie!' Hearing a hoarse cry, Lauren swung round. Mr Cassidy was running up the hill towards them, looking horrified. For a moment, Lauren felt a surge of hope but then her heart plummeted. It was obvious that Mr Cassidy couldn't move the log on his own. There was still only one way for Mel to get out and that was for Shadow to jump.

Twilight seemed to realize the same thing. Throwing his head back, he whinnied loudly to Shadow. As he did so, a fork of lightning flashed across the sky, making every hair of his grey body shine with a bright white light.

Suddenly, Lauren saw a new look of bravery flash into Shadow's eyes. Tossing his head back, just like Twilight, he broke into a canter. Mel grabbed hold of his mane with her free hand. Shadow's stride length-ened. His ears pricked and the next second he was soaring over the burning log, clearing it with ease.

Mel was hanging on to Midnight, a look of astonishment, relief and delight on her face as they galloped up to Twilight. 'He did it!' she said, sliding off Shadow's back as he halted.

'He was amazing!' Lauren cried, and Twilight whinnied in agreement.

Just then Mr Cassidy reached them. 'Mel!' he said, his breath coming in short gasps. 'I thought you weren't going to get out. What were you doing in the hay-barn?'

'Rescuing Midnight,' Mel stammered.

'But I told you not to leave the barn,' Mr Cassidy said, pulling her into his arms. 'I'm just so glad you're safe.'

'And it's all because of Shadow,' Mel said, breaking free and hugging the dapple-grey pony. 'Wasn't he wonderful, Dad?'

Mr Cassidy smiled at Shadow. 'The best.'

As the fire crew arrived and began to put out the fire, Mr Cassidy helped the girls make up a special feed of warm bran, carrots and molasses for Shadow and Twilight. Once the two ponies were dry and bedded down in two stalls, Lauren and Mel went inside.

As Lauren looked out of the kitchen to where the fire crew was saying goodbye to Mr Cassidy she breathed a sigh of relief. Luckily the flames hadn't spread to the barn, so Mr Cassidy's hay was OK.

In fact, Lauren thought, *everything has turned out OK.* She and Mel and both horses were safe. Midnight, the kitten, had been reunited with Sparkle and Mel had made the little family a new bed in the stall next to Shadow.

Lauren shivered as she realized that it could have all

been so different. If it hadn't been for Shadow's bravery, she didn't like to think what might have happened.

That night, when Lauren turned Twilight into a unicorn, she asked him if he knew how Shadow had found the courage to jump.

'No, I don't,' Twilight admitted. 'Shall we go and visit him to find out?'

Shadow was grazing near the bottom of his moonlit paddock.

'You were amazing today, Shadow,' Lauren said, as he whinnied a greeting. What made you able to jump?'

Shadow neighed.

'He says that when the lightning flashed it made me look like a unicorn. He realized that if he was going to save Mel, he had to be as brave as he was the other night when my horn touched him – as brave as a unicorn.'

Lauren nodded, remembering the look that had come into Shadow's eyes as the lightning had shone on Twilight's coat.

'You were wonderful, Shadow, and, best of all, now that you've jumped that great big log, the jumps at Pony Club will seem tiny. You'll be able to jump them easily.'

Shadow snorted doubtfully.

'He doesn't think so,' Twilight interpreted. 'He says that he could only jump the log because he had to.'

Lauren frowned. 'But Twilight wasn't a unicorn when you jumped that log, Shadow. You jumped that log because you were brave.'

Shadow stared at Lauren as if she'd said something totally astonishing.

'You saved Mel's life, Shadow,' Lauren said softly. 'If you can do that, you can do anything.'

A new look of confidence began to shine in Shadow's eyes.

He whinnied proudly and tossed his mane as Lauren rode Twilight off into the night.

On Saturday afternoon, Lauren stood beside Twilight, watching Mel ride Shadow towards the first jump in the course that Kathy, their Pony Club trainer, had set out.

'I don't know why Mel's bothering,' Jade's snide voice cut through the air. She was watching with Monica. 'Shadow's never going to jump.'

Lauren didn't say anything. She just crossed her fingers. The course was small but twisty and no one in the group had managed a clear round yet. She held her breath. Would Shadow stop?

But, to her delight, the dapple-grey pony's ears pricked up, his stride lengthened and he jumped perfectly over the fence. He cantered to the next one and then the next. As he cleared the last fence, everyone burst into applause for a perfect clear round.

Seeing the happiness on Mel's and Shadow's faces, Lauren hugged Twilight in delight. 'Oh, Twilight, isn't it brilliant?' she whispered. 'I'm so glad you were able to help.'

Twilight shook his head and pushed his nose against her chest.

Lauren understood him perfectly. 'OK then,' she said, putting her arm round his neck. 'I'm so glad *we* were able to help!'

Magical Unicorn Fun

Who will reach Twilight first –
Lauren, Buddy or
the little toy duck?

There are twelve magical words hidden in
this My Secret Unicorn wordsearch.
Can you find them?

(Remember that the words can run across or
down, diagonally and even backwards.)

R S A Y S N H L U T
S E N R L R A O H F
T R W G C U E G R C
A U O O R A I W I N
B T E E L L D G O Q
L N N S I F A I Z P
E E W W H M N P A Z
S V T U N I C O R N
D D S L L E P S O Z
V A P O N Y O K B M

ADVENTURES
ARCADIA
HORN
LAUREN
MAGIC
MOONFLOWER

PONY
POWERS
SPELLS
STABLES
TWILIGHT
UNICORN

Stronger Than Magic

Chapter One

'I love this place,' Lauren Foster whispered as she sat on Twilight's warm back. Fireflies danced around them, lighting up the dusky shadows of the peaceful forest glade.

Moonlight shone on Twilight's silvery horn as he nodded. 'Me too.'

Lauren patted him. She could hardly believe how lucky she was. Most of the time, Twilight looked like any ordinary grey pony, but when she said the words of the Turning Spell, he transformed into a magical unicorn and they flew to places like this secret glade in the woods.

'Shall we stay here or shall we fly some more?' asked Twilight.

Lauren glanced at her watch. 'We should really go home.'

Lauren's parents had no idea that Twilight was a unicorn. At the moment, they just thought she was outside in his paddock, feeding him.

'I could use my unicorn powers to see whether they're worrying,' Twilight suggested. 'If they aren't, we could stay out a little longer.'

'That's a great idea,' Lauren replied.

Twilight trotted over to one of the unusual rocks at the side of the clearing. As a unicorn, he had many magical powers. One of them allowed him to use the rocks of rose quartz to see what was happening anywhere else in the world. Touching his horn to the surface of one, he said, 'Granger's Farm!'

There was a bright purple flash and mist started to swirl. As it cleared, an image of Lauren's home – Granger's Farm – appeared in the rock. Lauren slid off Twilight's back to look more closely. She could see Twilight's paddock, the surrounding fields filled with cows, her bedroom window, her mum's car . . .

'Lauren's mum and dad,' Twilight said to the rock.

The picture wobbled and suddenly Mr and Mrs Foster appeared. They were talking, but all Lauren could hear was a faint buzz. Tucking her long, fair hair behind her ears, she leaned closer to the rock. The buzz turned into voices.

'Is Lauren still outside with Twilight?' she heard her dad say.

Lauren tensed, but to her relief her mum spoke calmly.

'She is, but don't worry. She knows to be in by bedtime. She just likes spending as much time with him as possible,' Mrs Foster said, smiling. 'It's one of the best things about having moved to the country. Lauren and Max can have so much more freedom. If we were still in the city . . .'

Lauren sat back on her heels. 'It's OK,' she said to Twilight. 'I think we're safe for a while.'

'Shall we do some flying then?' Twilight said eagerly.

'In a minute,' Lauren said. She was enjoying looking at her family. 'Can I have a look at Max first?'

'All right,' Twilight said obligingly. 'Max!' he said.

The picture focused to show Max, Lauren's six-year-old brother. He was playing with his Bernese mountain dog puppy, Buddy.

Lauren could tell from the way he was holding a dog treat in his hand that he was trying to get Buddy to sit.

She grinned at Twilight. 'Max and Buddy are starting dog-training classes tomorrow.' She watched the picture for a few more seconds. It was fun not being seen. 'Let's have a look at Mel now,' she said to Twilight. 'Just quickly.'

Mel Cassidy was Lauren's neighbour and one of her best friends. Twilight murmured Mel's name and the picture changed to show Mel sitting in her bedroom with her mum. Mrs Cassidy had her arm round Mel's shoulders.

'Mel's crying!' Lauren said in alarm. She started to lean forward and then stopped. Listening to her own family was one thing, but somehow listening in on a friend talking to her mum didn't seem right. 'I don't know if we should listen,' she said doubtfully.

'But perhaps if we know what's wrong, we can help,' Twilight pointed out.

Lauren hesitated for a moment. She and Twilight were good at helping people in trouble. That's why unicorns came to live in the human world – to use their magical powers to do good deeds with their human owners. She looked at the picture in the rock. Mel looked really upset. Quickly, Lauren made up her mind. 'OK, but we'll only listen for a second,' she said.

Lauren and Twilight leaned closer.

'It's not fair,' she heard Mel say. 'I just can't do it, Mum. I've asked Mr Noland to explain twice now and I still don't get it!'

'You'll just have to ask Mr Noland to go through it again,' Mrs Cassidy said gently.

Lauren frowned in surprise. Mr Noland was their class teacher. What could be upsetting Mel?

'But then Lauren and Jessica will think I'm really dumb!' Mel cried.

'I'm sure they won't,' Mrs Cassidy said, hugging her. 'They're your friends.'

'But they can do fractions. It's just me who can't!' Mel said.

Fractions! Lauren sat back and the voices faded to a buzz again.

'Fractions?' Twilight said, sounding puzzled. 'What are they?'

'They're something we're doing in maths,' Lauren answered.

'So it's nothing serious then,' Twilight said in relief.

'Well, I don't know.' Lauren hesitated. 'If Mel's upset by it, then it is serious. She seems to think Jessica and I will laugh at her.' She shook her head. 'But we'd never do that. We don't care if she can do fractions or not. She's our friend.' She chewed a fingernail. 'Poor Mel,' she said softly. 'I wish I could help her.'

Twilight looked doubtful. 'I don't think any of my magic powers can help people do maths.'

'I guess not,' Lauren said. 'It looks like this is one problem I'll have to solve on my own.'

Chapter Two

'Lauren! You're going to be late for school!' Mrs Foster called up the stairs the next morning.

Lauren pulled a brush through her hair and hurried downstairs. School mornings were always a rush. As she ran into the kitchen, she almost fell over Buddy.

'Sit, Buddy! Buddy, sit!' Max was saying.

Seeing Lauren, Buddy leapt up in delight. Lauren tickled his ears. 'Hey, boy,' she said.

'Buddy! Come here and sit!' Max commanded sternly as the puppy gambolled around Lauren's legs.

Buddy crouched down with his front legs and stuck his bottom playfully in the air. 'Woof!' he barked, before bounding off wildly around the kitchen.

'He's going to be just great at obedience classes, Max,' Lauren teased as Buddy skidded to a halt too late and cannoned into the fridge door. 'He'll be bottom of the class.'

'He won't!' Max cried. 'Mum!' He turned to their mum. 'He won't, will he?'

'Buddy will be just fine, honey,' Mrs Foster said reassuringly. 'Lauren, stop teasing Max and eat some breakfast.'

Lauren sat down and buttered a piece of toast. Max was trying to open a new jar of chocolate spread.

'Come on, Max,' Lauren said impatiently. 'We'll be late.'

Max twisted with all his

strength but the lid wouldn't come off.

'Here, let me,' Lauren said, taking it from him and opening it in one go.

'Lauren!' Max protested. 'I wanted to do it!'

'We'd have been here all morning,' Lauren told him.

'That's enough, both of you!' Mrs Foster said, running a hand through her hair. 'Finish your toast and let's go.'

'Hi, Lauren!' Jessica Parker called as Lauren ran into the classroom just before the bell rang.

'Hi,' Lauren said. She still hadn't thought of a plan to help Mel and it was troubling her.

Just then, Mel hurried into the classroom.

'Hi,' Lauren said.

'Hello,' Mel replied. Lauren noticed that her voice was much quieter than usual.

Before they could say anything else, the bell rang and Mr Noland came into the classroom. 'Quiet, please!' he said, clapping his hands.

As Mr Noland took the register, Lauren watched Mel. She was looking pale and unhappy.

'OK, everyone, maths books out, please,' Mr Noland said as he put the register away. 'I'd like you to work through exercise three on page twenty-two.'

They fetched their maths books and quiet fell as everyone began working. Lauren could see that Mel was staring at the page of fractions, a panicky look on her face.

'Are you stuck?' Lauren whispered to her. 'I can help if you like.'

'No . . . no, I'm just thinking,' Mel replied as she hastily scribbled down an answer.

'You don't seem to have done very much, Lauren.' Mr Noland's voice behind her made Lauren jump. 'Do you need some help?'

Lauren looked up guiltily. 'No, I'm fine . . .' she started to say but then she stopped. She'd had an idea. 'Actually, I do need help, please,' she said quickly. 'I'm confused.'

Mr Noland looked surprised. 'But you've been managing fractions OK all week. What seems to be the problem?' He leaned over her desk. 'All you have to do is put the fractions in order, smallest first. You need to consider both the denominator and the numerator —'

'The numerator is the number on top of the fraction and the denominator is the number on the bottom of the fraction, isn't it?' Lauren said, stopping him before he could race on ahead like he usually did.

'Yes and —'

'A fraction is just a small part of a whole, isn't it, Mr Noland?' Lauren said quickly. 'Like one piece of a whole cake. The denominator — the bottom number — tells you how many pieces the cake has been cut into and the numerator — the top number — tells you how many pieces of cake you have.' She glanced quickly to the side and was relieved to see that Mel was listening.

'Yes, that's right,' said Mr Noland, starting to sound a bit impatient.

'So, if the fraction is one third — one over three — the denominator is three which means the cake has been cut into three pieces,' she went on.

'Yes,' Mr Noland replied. 'And if you see the fraction one fifth — one over five — the denominator is . . . ?'

Before Lauren could answer, Mel spoke up. 'Five?'

Lauren and Mr Noland looked round.

'That's right, Mel,' Mr Noland said.

'Which means the cake has been cut into five pieces. And the fraction one tenth would mean the cake had been cut into ten pieces,'

Mel said, her eyes starting to light up. 'One fifth is bigger than one tenth because if you cut a cake into five pieces, each slice of the cake is bigger than if you'd cut it into ten pieces.'

'That's right,' Mr Noland said to her.

Mel's eyes were shining. 'It suddenly all makes sense.'

'Well, that's great,' Mr Noland said. 'How about you, Lauren? Do you understand now?'

'Me?' Lauren caught herself. 'Oh, yes. Thank you, Mr Noland.'

Mr Noland smiled. 'Well, I'm glad you're happier.'

Lauren looked at the relief on Mel's face and smiled. 'Yes,' she said, feeling warm inside. 'I'm much happier now!'

Lauren was still glowing when she got home after school. 'You should have seen Mel's face when she finally worked out fractions,' she told Twilight as she groomed him before tacking him up to take him out on a ride with Mel and her pony, Shadow. 'She looked so relieved.'

Twilight snorted. When he was a pony he couldn't talk to her, but Lauren knew he understood every word she said.

'It kind of made me think,' Lauren said as she cleaned out the curry-comb. 'I know we try and help people when they've got big problems – like the time we helped Jessica when she was really upset about her dad getting remarried, but couldn't we also use your powers to help those with smaller problems too? Sometimes people get almost as upset over something little as over something big.' She looked at Twilight. He looked as though he was listening hard. 'What do you think?'

Twilight nodded his head.

Lauren hugged him. 'It'll be evening soon,' she whispered. 'We can talk properly then.'

Chapter Three

'I'm just going out to see Twilight, Mum,' Lauren said, pulling her trainers on after supper.

'OK, honey,' Mrs Foster replied. She stood up and looked over to where Max was playing with Buddy. 'Come on, Max, time for your bath.'

Lauren ran down to the paddock. She couldn't wait to find out what Twilight thought of her plan about helping people with little problems as well as big.

'So, what do you think?' she asked as soon as he was a unicorn again.

'It's a good idea,' Twilight answered. 'The more people we can help, the better.'

Lauren grinned in delight. 'I was hoping you'd say that!'

'There are some rocks of rose quartz over there,' Twilight said, nodding in the direction of a cluster of trees at the end of his paddock. 'We could check who needs help right now.'

'OK!' Lauren mounted and they cantered down the paddock. Not for the first time, Lauren felt thankful that Twilight's paddock was well hidden from the house. She and Twilight should be safe in the shadow of the trees.

'There they are,' Twilight said, pointing his horn at several small boulders under an oak tree.

'Let's see Mel first,' Lauren said eagerly.

Within a few seconds, a picture had appeared in the rock, showing Mel snuggled up to her mum on the sofa.

'She looks much happier,' Twilight said, pleased.

Lauren nodded. 'OK, let's try Jessica.'

Twilight said Jessica's name and the picture changed. Jessica was sitting in the kitchen talking to her dad. She was frowning.

Lauren leaned forward to find out why Jessica was looking so miserable.

'But I really wanted a pony, Dad,' Jessica was saying.

'It'll be easier to find one in the summer holidays,' Mr Parker replied. 'We'll have more time.'

Lauren sighed. She knew Jessica wanted a pony right now, but she didn't see how she and Twilight could help with that. She was about to ask him to look at someone else when Jessica said something that caught her attention.

'But I get left out, Dad,' she said. 'Lauren and Mel meet after school to go riding together and I can't join in. Like this afternoon, they went riding together and I couldn't go with them.'

Lauren sat back. 'Did you hear that?'

Twilight nodded. 'It can't be much fun for Jessica seeing you and Mel riding together.' He shook his mane. 'But it's easy to solve. When you and Mel next meet up, ask Jessica to join you. You can take it in turns to ride me and Shadow.'

'Good idea,' Lauren said. Fired up by thinking how easy it would be to solve Jessica's unhappiness, she looked at the rock again. 'OK, let's see if anyone else in my class is unhappy.' She started suggesting different names. A little niggling feeling ran through her. She knew she shouldn't really be listening in on other people's conversations. Still, it was for the best, wasn't it? It was so she could help them.

Lauren got so engrossed in seeing the other kids from her class going about their everyday lives – watching TV, reading, doing homework – that she almost forgot that she was supposed to be looking for someone who was unhappy. She was relieved – everyone seemed to be doing just fine. She glanced at her watch.

'I hadn't realized it was so late.' She stood up. 'We've only got ten minutes before I have to go in. We'll just have time to have a very quick fly-round tonight.'

'Let's go then,' Twilight said, touching his horn to the rock and making the picture disappear. Lauren mounted and held on to his mane.

Twilight started to trot forward, but then suddenly stopped. 'I feel tired,' he said, sounding surprised.

'Tired?' Lauren echoed.

'Yes, sort of achy but . . . but . . .' Twilight looked confused. 'It's strange – I never normally feel tired when I'm a unicorn.'

'We don't have to fly tonight,' Lauren said, concerned. 'Maybe you're not well.'

'No, I'll be fine,' Twilight replied bravely. 'Let's try again.' He trotted forward and this time took off into the sky. Lauren felt the cool wind streaming against her face. She leaned forward. They were flying again!

But soon she started to feel worried. Twilight seemed to be going slower than usual. Normally he galloped and swooped lightly and easily, but tonight his movements felt heavy and slow.

'Are you OK?' she asked.

'I . . . I feel a little strange,' Twilight replied.

'Let's go down,' Lauren said quickly.

Twilight didn't argue. Turning, he flew back to the paddock.

As he landed, Lauren slid off his back. He was breathing heavily. 'What's wrong?' she asked.

'I don't know,' he answered.

'Maybe you're coming down with some sort of bug,' Lauren said anxiously. 'Shall I get Dad to call the vet?'

Twilight shook his head. 'I don't feel ill. Just tired. I'll probably be better in the morning.'

'I'll turn you back into a pony and make you a warm bran mash,' Lauren said. 'That might help.'

Twilight nodded and Lauren said the Undoing Spell. Then, going to the feed room, she put several scoops of bran, a handful of oats and some salt into a bucket and added hot water. Mixing it all up, she carried it back to Twilight. 'Here, boy, eat this.'

Twilight whickered gratefully and plunged his nose into the bucket.

As he ate, Lauren kissed his head. *Oh, Twilight*, she thought, biting her lip, *please be OK*.

Chapter Four

Lauren didn't sleep well that night. As soon as she woke up, she looked out of her window. Twilight was standing by the gate. Pulling on her clothes, Lauren hurried outside.

'Are you feeling better now?' she asked.

To her relief, Twilight nodded.

Lauren rubbed his forehead. 'I've been so worried,' she told him softly. 'I don't think I could bear you to be ill.'

'Do you want to go for a ride this evening?' Mel asked Lauren as they got their books out that morning.

'Yes – if Twilight's OK,' Lauren replied.

'What's the matter with him?' Jessica asked, looking concerned.

'He didn't seem very well last night,' Lauren said. 'He was tired.'

'Maybe he's got a cold,' Mel suggested. 'Shadow sometimes gets them. They make him a bit quiet, but they're not serious. So, do you want to meet up?' she asked. 'We could ride at mine instead of going out, then, if Twilight seems tired, you can always go home.'

'OK,' Lauren replied. She happened to glance at Jessica and caught a look of unhappiness fleeting across her face. 'Hey, Jess,' Lauren said quickly, 'why don't you meet us as well? We can take it in turns to ride.'

'Yeah,' Mel said, looking at Jessica. 'That's a great idea.'

'Really? Are you sure you don't mind?' Jessica said hesitantly.

'Of course not,' Lauren told her and Mel shook her head.

'OK then,' Jessica said, smiling. 'Thanks. I'll see if Dad will drop me off.'

To Lauren's relief, Twilight seemed to be back to his normal self when she got home from school that afternoon. He whinnied when he saw her coming.

'Do you feel well enough to go round to Mel's?' she asked him.

Twilight nodded. Feeling much happier, Lauren groomed him and saddled up.

Jessica was already at Mel's house when Lauren and Twilight arrived and the three girls had lots of fun timing themselves as they took it in turns to ride Shadow and Twilight around an obstacle course in Shadow's paddock.

'I've had a great time,' Jessica said happily as they let the ponies graze afterwards while they ate home-made cookies.

'We'll have to do this again,' Lauren said. 'It's more fun when there are three of us.'

'Yeah, definitely,' Mel said. 'Until you get your own pony, you can ride Shadow as much as you like, Jess.'

'And Twilight,' Lauren said.

Jessica's eyes shone happily. 'Thanks, guys. You're the best friends ever!'

'Jessica really enjoyed herself today,' Lauren said to Twilight that night after she had turned him into a unicorn.

'I'm glad we found out that she was upset,' Twilight said.

Lauren nodded. 'Let's have a look and see if there's anyone else who needs our help.'

They went down to the end of the field where the rose-quartz rocks were. The first person Lauren and Twilight saw was a boy in her class, David Andrews, with his father.

'They look like they're arguing,' Lauren said, leaning closer to the rock.

'I'm not going to wear them!' David was saying.

101

'Yes, you are,' his dad replied firmly. 'And I've written to Mr Noland asking him to make sure that you do.'

'Dad!' David cried.

'It's for the best,' his dad said. He shook his head. 'David, lots of people wear glasses . . .'

Lauren looked at Twilight. 'Glasses!' she exclaimed. 'That's all that's upsetting David – he's got to wear glasses.'

'Well, if you tell him how good his glasses look, it might help,' Twilight suggested.

'It's worth a try,' Lauren agreed. 'Come on, let's look at some other people.'

Most of the other kids seemed happy enough, apart from Joanne Bailey. Joanne sat at the table next to Lauren and she was miserable because her computer had broken down. She couldn't do the geography research that Mr Noland had asked them to do by the next day.

'I can easily help with that,' Lauren said. 'I'll print out some extra research from the Internet and take it in tomorrow for Joanne to use –'

'Lauren,' Twilight interrupted. 'I . . . I feel strange again.'

Lauren looked at him in concern. 'It's my fault. I shouldn't have

made you do that obstacle course at Mel's.'

'But I was feeling all right then,' Twilight said. 'It's just now – I feel tired all of a sudden.' He shook his head wearily. 'Can we stop doing the magic now? I think I'd better change back.'

'Of course,' Lauren said, jumping to her feet.

Once Twilight was a pony again, he lay down. Lauren watched him, feeling very worried. What was the matter with him? He was never tired or ill. And this was twice now in two days.

'I'll leave my window open tonight,' she whispered. 'Whinny if you want anything and I'll come straight down.'

Twilight snorted softly and closed his eyes.

Lauren kept her window open all night just as she had promised. At six o'clock, she jumped out of bed and crossed the room to look out. But Twilight wasn't by the gate. Lauren felt alarmed. Twilight always stood there in the morning. Pulling on her jeans, she hurried outside.

As she reached the paddock, she saw Twilight still lying where she had left him. His nose was resting heavily on the ground and his eyes were closed.

'Twilight!' Lauren cried out.

Twilight's ears flickered and he half-raised his head. He looked exhausted.

Lauren scrambled over the gate and raced across the grass. Throwing herself down on the ground beside him, she touched his neck. 'Twilight!' she gasped. 'What's the matter? You look really ill!'

Twilight snorted weakly.

'I'm going to get Dad!' Lauren said, jumping to her feet. 'Don't worry, Twilight. I'll be back as soon as I can.'

Chapter Five

Mr Foster was very worried when he saw Twilight. 'I'm going to call the vet,' he said.

As he hurried off, Lauren crouched down beside her pony. 'You're going to be OK,' she told him, her eyes stinging with hot tears. 'We'll find out what's wrong with you, I promise.'

Tony Blackstone, their vet, arrived within the hour. He took Twilight's temperature and monitored his heart rate, then he ran his hands all over Twilight's body.

'Has Twilight been off-colour for a while?' he asked Lauren.

'He seemed tired the day before yesterday,' she replied, 'but otherwise he's been fine.'

'So he hasn't had a cough, or runny nose, or been restless and wanting to roll?'

'No,' Lauren replied.

Tony continued his examination, but at last he shook his head. 'Well, it's puzzling. If it weren't for the way he's acting, I'd say he seems to be a very healthy pony. I'll take a blood test and see what shows up. Maybe he's got a virus.'

'Is there anything we can do?' Mr Foster asked.

'Call me if he gets any worse, but otherwise just let him rest. I'll ring you with the test results as soon as I have them.' Tony shot Lauren a comforting glance. 'Don't worry. I'm sure he's going to be just fine.'

Lauren thought about Twilight all the way to school. What if there was something seriously wrong with him? A cold feeling clenched at her heart.

Walking into the cloakroom, she saw Joanne Bailey talking to her friend, Rachel. Lauren suddenly remembered about the extra

research that she had printed out. 'Hi,' she said to them, as she put her coat on the peg. 'Did you do the geography homework last night?'

'Yeah,' Rachel replied.

'I couldn't,' Joanne said. 'My computer broke down.'

'I've got some extra if you need some more,' Lauren offered eagerly.

'It's OK, thanks,' Joanne replied. 'Rachel's lent me some of hers.'

'Are you sure?' Lauren asked, taking out the papers. 'I have them right here.'

'No, really, I'm fine,' Joanne said, and turned back to continue her conversation with Rachel.

Feeling disappointed that her plan to help hadn't worked out as she'd hoped, Lauren went into the classroom. As she walked through the door, she saw David talking with a group of his friends. She stopped. David had his new glasses on but, to her relief, his friends didn't seem to be teasing him.

Just then, David glanced up and caught her watching him. 'What are you looking at?' he asked suspiciously.

'Nothing,' Lauren replied.

'It must be your glasses,' one of David's friends sniggered.

'It isn't!' Lauren said quickly, seeing David go red. 'They're . . . they're very nice glasses.'

David's friends burst out laughing.

'Lauren likes you, David!' one of them said.

'Lauren Foster wants to be your girlfriend.'

'No, I don't!' Lauren exclaimed.

She hurried to her desk, her own cheeks burning. As she went, she could hear David's friends start to tease him about how girls really liked boys with glasses. *Oh, great*, Lauren thought in dismay. *I haven't helped David at all – in fact, it looks like I've made things worse!*

To her relief, Mel and Jessica arrived and she didn't have to listen to David's friends any more.

After school, Lauren went straight to see Twilight. To her relief, he whinnied when he saw her and trotted over to the gate. Lauren's heart rose. He looked much happier.

She got out her grooming kit and spent ages brushing him and combing out every tangle in his mane and tail. As she worked, she told him about David and Joanne. 'They didn't seem to need my help,' she said. 'In fact, I think I made things worse for David by saying that his glasses were nice. His friends started teasing him then.' She sighed. 'I wish you could talk back, but I won't turn you into a unicorn tonight. You've got to rest.'

Twilight nuzzled her.

'I'm going to go and get you some carrots,' Lauren said. 'I'll be back in a minute.'

She hurried to the house. Her dad was in the kitchen with Max. They had just got back from dog-training class and Max was putting Buddy's lead away.

Lauren took three carrots from the fridge. Buddy came over to see what she was doing. She patted him. 'How was Buddy's lesson?'

Buddy tried to put his head on Max's knee, but Max pushed him away.

Mr Foster sighed. 'Buddy wasn't very good today,' he explained to Lauren. 'They were trying to teach the puppies to fetch a toy, but Buddy just kept running off and not coming back.'

Max stared at the floor.

'Don't worry,' Lauren said sympathetically. 'I'm sure Buddy will learn soon.'

'Lauren's right, Max,' Mr Foster said. 'You've got all weekend to teach Buddy how to fetch. There isn't another class until Monday.'

Lauren bent down and stroked the puppy. 'He'll learn to fetch, won't you, Buddy?'

Looking up at her, Buddy wagged his tail.

The next morning, Tony Blackstone came to check on Twilight again. 'Nothing obvious has shown up on the blood test,' he told Lauren and Mr Foster, 'but I'll send it off to the lab for further analysis. Still, I'm sure there's nothing to worry about. He looks better already, don't you, boy?'

Twilight whickered.

Tony smiled. 'You'd almost think he could understand what I was saying.'

Lauren only just managed to hide her grin. *If only he knew!* 'Should he rest today?' she asked.

'Yes, just to be on the safe side,' Tony said.

As Mr Foster walked with the vet back to his car, Max picked up a stick and threw it. 'Go, boy!' he called to Buddy. 'Go fetch!'

Buddy bounded up to the stick and grabbed it.

'That's it! Bring it here, Buddy!' Max called.

Buddy wagged his tail, the stick firmly clenched in his teeth.

'Buddy, come here!' Max said, his voice rising in exasperation. He started to walk towards the puppy, but Buddy dodged around Max and gambolled away up the path.

'Buddy!' Max shouted crossly. 'Come back!'

But Buddy ignored him and galloped out of sight.

'You could try keeping him on a lead,' Lauren suggested as Max stared after him. 'Then he couldn't get away.'

'I *know* how to train him, Lauren,' Max snapped. 'You don't need to tell me.'

'I was only trying to help,' Lauren told him.

'Well, I don't need your help!' Max said. 'I –'

Mrs Foster appeared at the top of the path. 'Max!' she interrupted them. 'Can you go and get your swimming things, please? We don't want to be late.'

Max ran off as Mrs Foster walked down to Lauren. 'Do you want to come into town with us, honey?'

Lauren shook her head. 'I'll stay here with Twilight.'

'OK,' her mum said. 'Dad's around. If you need anything, just ask.'

After her mum and Max had driven away, Lauren groomed Twilight and then set to work cleaning his tack and tidying the tack room. By mid-morning everything was spotless.

Lauren went down to the paddock where Twilight was grazing. She sighed. There wasn't much else she could do. Unless . . .

Lauren looked round. Her dad was out on the farm and there was no one else nearby. If she turned Twilight into a unicorn, they could at least talk. Maybe they could even look to see if there were some more people to help. That wouldn't be too tiring. All he'd have to do was touch his horn to a rock.

She led Twilight to the shadow of the trees and said the magic words.

'So, how are you feeling?' she asked as soon as Twilight was a unicorn again.

'Not too bad,' Twilight answered. 'Just a bit weak and . . .' He pawed at the ground with his hoof. 'Anyway, I'm feeling better than I did yesterday.'

'I was so frightened,' Lauren said. 'I thought you were terribly ill.' She looked towards the bottom of the field. 'Can we go and use your magic powers? I want to see if there's anyone else I can help.' She sighed. 'I didn't exactly do that well with David and Joanne yesterday.'

'At least you tried,' Twilight said reassuringly.

'I guess,' Lauren said as they went over to one of the rocks.

'When will your mum and Max be back?' Twilight asked.

'Probably not for ages yet,' Lauren replied. 'But we could check and see where they are just to be on the safe side.'

Twilight nodded and, touching his horn to a rock, he murmured, 'Mrs Foster and Max.'

The picture in the rock showed Mrs Foster and Max having a drink in town. Lauren leaned closer. 'I'm never going to get Buddy to fetch,' Max was saying.

'Oh, Max!' Mrs Foster said. 'You've only been trying for one day. Just be patient.'

'Poor Max,' Lauren said to Twilight. 'He's really unhappy that Buddy won't –' She broke off. 'I've had an idea!' she said, her eyes widening. 'Why don't I teach Buddy to fetch? Just think how pleased Max would be to get back and find that Buddy could do it after all!'

Twilight didn't answer. He was rubbing his head against his leg as if it hurt.

Lauren looked at him in concern. 'Are you OK?'

'I'm feeling strange,' Twilight replied weakly. 'I think I need to rest.'

'I'll turn you back,' Lauren said immediately.

As soon as Twilight was a pony again he sighed and half-shut his eyes.

Lauren stroked his face. 'Do you want anything?'

Twilight shook his head.

'OK,' Lauren said. 'Well, I'll be by the stable with Buddy. If you need me, just whinny.'

She went to find Buddy. The puppy was asleep in the kitchen. He got up eagerly when Lauren came in.

'Come on, boy,' Lauren said, taking a packet of dog treats, a long dog lead and a toy from the cupboard. 'I'm going to teach you to fetch.'

Taking Buddy outside, she clipped on his lead. 'I'm going to throw this toy,' she told him. 'And I want you to bring it back.'

Buddy woofed in excitement as he looked at the orange plastic duck in her hand.

'Go on then, boy,' Lauren said, throwing the toy. 'Go fetch!'

Buddy raced after the duck, grabbed it and then, just as he had done with Max, he started to bound away. But this time, the lead pulled him up short. He stopped in surprise and shook his head.

Lauren held out a dog treat. 'Here, boy,' she encouraged.

Buddy looked at her and tried to back off but the lead held him tight.

Lauren waved the dog treat. 'Come on, Buddy.'

Buddy hesitated for a moment and then seemed to make up his mind. Still holding the toy, he trotted over to her.

'Good boy!' Lauren cried as he dropped the plastic duck and eagerly gobbled up the treat. She made a fuss of him and then stood up. 'OK. Let's try that again.'

Twenty minutes later, Buddy had got the hang of fetching the toy. As soon as he picked it up, he carried it back to Lauren, knowing that a treat was waiting for him.

'You are *such* a clever boy,' Lauren praised him after he had done it without the lead attached. 'Max is going to be so pleased!'

Buddy wagged his tail and, leaving him to play, Lauren went back to check on Twilight.

He was lying down in the paddock. Lauren knelt down beside him. 'Twilight? How are you feeling? Shall I get Dad to call the vet?'

Twilight shook his head and rested his muzzle on her knees.

'Oh, Twilight,' Lauren said. 'I wish I knew what the matter was.' She massaged his ears and he sighed.

Lauren wasn't sure how long she'd been sitting with Twilight when the silence was broken by the sound of Max's voice.

'Buddy! Where are you?' Max came running down the path to the paddock. Buddy woofed in delight and bounded over to say hello.

Seeing Twilight lying down, Max stopped in concern. 'Is Twilight sick again, Lauren?'

Lauren stood up. Her legs felt stiff from sitting on the ground for so long. 'He just seems tired.'

'Poor Twilight,' Max said. 'I hope he gets better soon.' He patted Buddy. 'Come on, Buddy. Now that I'm back I'm going to teach you to fetch.'

Lauren remembered her good news. 'You don't have to,' she said, smiling.

'What do you mean?' Max said in surprise.

'I taught him while you were out. Watch this.' Seeing the toy duck lying by the gate, Lauren picked it up and threw it. 'Fetch, Buddy!'

Buddy trotted over, picked the duck up and brought it back. 'Good boy!' Lauren exclaimed, feeding him a dog treat from her pocket.

She turned to Max, her eyes shining. 'What do you think?'

To her surprise, she saw Max was frowning crossly at her. 'But Buddy's my dog. I wanted to teach him!' he cried.

'I was just trying to help,' Lauren said.

'No, you weren't.' Max looked close to tears. 'You just wanted to show that you could do it and I couldn't!'

'Max –' Lauren began.

But Max wouldn't listen. 'You always interfere, Lauren! You always ruin things!' Pushing past her, he ran off into the woods at the side of the paddock.

Lauren watched him go, feeling awful. She wanted Max to be pleased. She hadn't meant to upset him. But now that she thought about it, she could see what he meant. Perhaps training Buddy hadn't been a good idea. How would she feel if someone had done the same thing with Twilight? She wondered whether to go after him, but decided it was best to leave him until he'd calmed down.

With a sigh, she turned and went to find her mum to tell her about Twilight.

'I'll call Tony,' Mrs Foster said, looking at Twilight lying down in his field. 'Have you been riding this morning?'

'No, we just –' Lauren broke off. 'Well, we just stayed in the field.'

'So there's no reason why he should be tired,' Mrs Foster said.

Lauren shook her head. All Twilight had done that morning was some magic. A thought struck her and she almost gasped out loud. *Magic!* Of course! Why hadn't she thought about it before?

Chapter Six

Lauren's thoughts raced. Every time Twilight had started feeling strange, he had been in his unicorn form doing magic. Maybe he had some sort of special unicorn illness. That would explain why Tony Blackstone couldn't find anything wrong with him!

As her mum went back to the house to ring the vet, Lauren ran to Twilight. 'Twilight!' she said urgently.

Twilight looked up.

'I've had an idea. Maybe it's not the pony bit of you that's sick,' she said, 'maybe it's the *unicorn* bit! You always seem to be ill just after we've done some magic.'

Twilight looked thoughtful but Lauren couldn't tell exactly what he was thinking. She was filled with frustration. If only she could turn him into a unicorn and ask him what he thought, but she couldn't. Not in the middle of his field in broad daylight with her mum around. Then she had an idea.

'Maybe my book on unicorns will have something on unicorn illnesses,' she said. 'After all, that's where I found the words for the Turning Spell.'

Twilight bowed his head, as if in agreement.

'I'll be back later,' she said, almost running into her mum coming in the opposite direction.

'What's the matter?' her mum said in alarm. 'Has Twilight got worse?'

'No,' Lauren said. 'There's no change in him.'

'Well, I spoke to Tony,' her mum said. 'He's out on call at the moment and can't come over, but he said he'll ring in a few hours and see if there's any improvement.'

Lauren nodded. 'Thanks, Mum.' And before her mum could ask her what she was doing she raced on to the house and up to her bedroom. There she picked up the battered blue book lying by her bed and sat down. She knew the first chapter about Noah and the unicorns almost by heart now, but maybe one of the others might have something useful in them. Opening the book at the second chapter, she started to read.

Half an hour later, a knock at the door made her look up. 'Lauren?' her mum said, looking round the door. 'Have you seen Max?'

'No.' Lauren's head was swirling with unicorn facts. 'No, I haven't.'

'He must be outside somewhere with Buddy,' Mrs Foster said. 'I'll call him. It'll be lunchtime in five minutes.'

Lauren nodded. She just had a few more pages to read.

Mrs Foster left and Lauren turned back to the last chapter. She hadn't found out anything about unicorn illnesses and she was starting to feel increasingly desperate. The last chapter was all about what unicorns did on Earth. Lauren skimmed over the words. She knew most of it already. She read the last paragraph.

Magic is a very powerful force. It must be used wisely or it will exact a powerful toll. Only when a unicorn's powers are used to help those who are truly in need, will the unicorn be strengthened and his powers replenished.

Lauren frowned at the words. What did they mean? She thought she understood the last sentence – if Twilight did good, then he would become stronger. Well, that was all right. They'd been doing loads of good recently. He should be extra strong.

Lauren sighed and shut the book. She'd found out absolutely nothing about unicorns getting ill. Maybe they didn't get sick. Maybe her idea had been wrong after all.

She walked slowly downstairs. As she went into the

kitchen, she stopped in surprise. She'd been expecting to see Max and her mum sitting at the table ready to eat lunch. But there was no sign of Max, and her mum was standing by the sink, looking worried.

'I can't find Max anywhere,' Mrs Foster said. 'When did you last see him?'

'It was just after you got back from swimming,' Lauren replied. Just then, she remembered the argument and her cheeks flushed. 'We had a bit of a fight.'

'What sort of a fight?' her mum asked quickly.

'I'd taught Buddy to fetch while you were out,' Lauren said. 'I was just trying to help but Max got really cross and ran off. I didn't mean to upset him, Mum.'

'Oh, Lauren,' Mrs Foster sighed. 'I understand, but I can see why Max got angry. It's hard for him being the youngest. Sometimes it must seem to him as if you do everything before him. Training Buddy is the first thing he's ever done on his own.'

'I know. I should have realized,' Lauren said regretfully.

'I'd better call Dad,' Mrs Foster said. 'Perhaps Max is with him.'

Lauren watched anxiously as her mum made the call. She could tell from her face that it wasn't good news.

Mrs Foster replaced the receiver. 'Your dad hasn't seen Max. He's coming back to help us look.' She twisted her hands together. 'Which way did Max go when he ran off, Lauren?'

'Into the woods,' Lauren replied.

'That must have been about an hour and a half ago,' Mrs Foster said, checking her watch. 'I'll try ringing his friends. Maybe he went to one of their houses. Otherwise we'd better start searching.'

None of Max's friends had seen him, and when Mr Foster got back he and two of the farmhands, Tom and Hank, set out to look in the woods.

'Max could be anywhere,' Mrs Foster said to Lauren. 'He could still be walking or he might be hiding or . . .' her voice faltered, 'he might be hurt.'

'It'll be OK, Mum,' Lauren said quickly. An idea had come to her.

Mrs Foster nodded and took a deep breath. 'Yes, you're right,' she said, as if she were trying to convince herself, 'It will.' She shook her head. 'Oh, if only we knew which direction he'd gone. I just want him home.'

'I . . . I'm just going to see Twilight,' Lauren said.

Mrs Foster nodded distractedly. 'I'll stay by the phone.'

Lauren ran down to Twilight's field. Twilight had stood up and was by the gate.

'Twilight!' Lauren burst out. 'I know you're not well, but Max has run away and no one knows where he is – I really need your help. Please can I turn you into a unicorn? It would just be for a few minutes so that you can use your magic to see if we can find out where Max is. I wouldn't ask but . . .'

Twilight was already nodding his head up and down.

'Oh, thank you!' Lauren gasped.

Twilight started to trot to the trees. Lauren ran after him. As soon as they reached the safety of the shadows, Lauren said the magic words.

As she spoke the last line of the verse, she tensed expectantly.

There was a pause. For one awful moment, Lauren thought that the spell wasn't going to work, but then there was a weak purple flash and Twilight was suddenly a unicorn again.

'I thought you weren't going to change,' Lauren said, her heart pounding.

'Let's not worry about it now,' Twilight said quickly. 'We need to find out where Max is.' He touched his horn to the nearest rose-quartz rock. 'I want to see Max!'

Lauren and Twilight waited. They looked at each other.

Nothing had happened!

Chapter Seven

'It hasn't worked,' Lauren said, looking round. 'Maybe it's the wrong sort of rock. Try that one.' She pointed desperately to another.

Twilight trotted over. 'Max!' he said, touching his horn to the hard surface.

Again, nothing. Lauren looked horrified.

'Your magic's not working!' she exclaimed.

Twilight looked totally bewildered. 'I don't feel right. I feel drained, as if –' he looked at her in alarm – 'as if all my magic's been used up.'

His words sent a shock through Lauren. 'Used up? But it can't be!'

'That's how it feels,' Twilight said.

'But the unicorn book said that when unicorns do good they get stronger and their magic gets replenished,' Lauren said. 'We've been doing lots of good deeds. You should have loads of magic.'

'What did it say *exactly*?' Twilight asked urgently.

Lauren tried to remember. 'It was something about how a unicorn's magic mustn't be used lightly. I'll go and get it!'

She raced back to the house and returned a few minutes later with the book. 'Here,' she said, and she read out the last paragraph.

Magic is a very powerful force. It must be used wisely or it will exact a powerful toll. Only when a unicorn's

powers are used to help those who are truly in need will the unicorn be strengthened and —

She broke off with a gasp. 'Oh no! That's it!'

'What?' Twilight demanded.

'Don't you see?' Lauren said, pointing to the book. 'We've been trying to help everyone with all their little everyday problems, not people who are truly in need, so your magic hasn't been strengthened, it's just been used up. A toll is something you pay; well, maybe you're having to pay for how we've been using your magic. Maybe that's why you've been feeling ill!'

Twilight stared at her. 'You might be right.'

Tears sprang to Lauren's eyes. 'What are we going to do? Now we really need your magic to help find Max, we can't use it because there's none left.'

Twilight nuzzled her. 'Don't worry. We can still help to find Max even if we can't use my magic. There must be another way.'

He pawed at the ground, as if trying to think. A stick cracked beneath his hoof. 'I know what to do!' he said suddenly. 'Get Buddy and see if he can find Max. Pretend it's hide and seek. Buddy is brilliant at that!'

'Of course!' Lauren exclaimed.

'Turn me back into a pony and we can follow him to Max together,' Twilight said.

Lauren looked at Twilight in concern. 'But you're not well. You're too weak.'

'I don't care,' Twilight said, looking determined. 'I want to help you find your brother.'

'Are you sure?' Lauren said.

'Yes,' Twilight insisted. He nudged her with his nose. 'Come on, we're wasting time!'

Lauren didn't argue with him any longer. She turned him back into a pony, then she went into the house to tell her mother her plan, before fetching Buddy.

'We're going to find Max,' she told the puppy. She saddled Twilight and led him and Buddy to the place where she had last seen Max.

'Find Max, boy,' she said to Buddy. 'Good dog. Off you go.'

Buddy put his nose to the ground and began to snuffle round. Suddenly he seemed to pick up Max's scent. With a woof, he bounded up the path and into the woods. Lauren mounted Twilight and they trotted after him.

Lauren's heart was beating fast as they entered the trees. What if this idea didn't work? What if they all got lost trying to find Max? She pushed the thoughts out of her mind and concentrated on encouraging Buddy.

'That's it!' she called to the puppy. 'Good boy!'

Buddy set off down a narrow trail away from the main path. Lauren had to duck under low-hanging branches as the path twisted and turned. Brambles caught at her jeans.

She frowned as she tried to work out where they were. They seemed to be heading in the direction of . . .

The gorge!

'Buddy! Be careful!' she gasped in alarm. 'The path ends just ahead. It's dangerous!'

But Buddy started to run even faster. He disappeared from sight.

Lauren wondered what to do, but Twilight took the decision out of her hands. Breaking into a canter, he set off through the trees after the puppy. Lauren flung herself down against his neck. Clinging to Twilight's mane, she looked ahead as best she could.

Suddenly Lauren heard Buddy bark and then Twilight jerked to a stop. Her breath came in short gasps as she pushed herself upright in the saddle. Buddy was just ahead of them. He was standing beside a faded wooden sign that read:

DANGER
KEEP BACK

Her heart pounding, Lauren dismounted.

Twilight nuzzled her arm and she could tell he was also worried. Slipping the reins over her arm, she walked cautiously forward. She didn't dare walk right to the edge of the gorge in case the crumbling ground gave way. Letting go of Twilight, she dropped to her hands and knees and crawled the last few metres. She felt sick. What was she going to see when she looked over?

'Buddy!' she called as Buddy inched right to the edge. 'Be careful!'

'Lauren!' a faint voice called.

Lauren felt her heart leap. 'Max!' she gasped.

Chapter Eight

Throwing herself on to her stomach, she looked over the edge of the gorge. Max was crouched on a rocky ledge about four metres below the cliff edge. Beneath him, the gorge tumbled away steeply, ending in a pit of rocks and brambles far, far below. His eyes were wide with fear.

'Lauren,' he cried. 'You found me! I didn't think anyone ever would.'

'Are you OK?' Lauren asked.

'Yes. I was having a look over the side of the gorge and the ground just sort of crumbled,' Max said. 'But I landed on this ledge. I'm OK. I just can't get back up.'

Lauren went cold as she thought about what might have happened if he hadn't landed on the outcrop.

'I'll go and get help!' she said.

'No! Don't leave me!' Max looked terrified.

Lauren looked desperately at her brother. 'I've got to go. I can't reach you.'

'I don't want to stay here alone,' Max said tearfully.

'But you wouldn't be alone,' Lauren said desperately. 'Buddy's here.'

'Buddy!' Max gasped in delight. Buddy barked, as if in reply.

'Look, I'm going to have to go and get Mum and Dad, Max,' Lauren said. 'Buddy will

121

stay with you.'

Max looked up. 'OK,' he said bravely.

'I'll be back as soon as I can,' Lauren promised.

Edging away from the cliff, she stood up, commanded Buddy to stay and ran to Twilight. 'Quick, Twilight!' she gasped as she mounted. 'We've got to get home!'

'Lauren! Where have you been? I've been out of my mind with worry!' Mrs Foster came running down the path as Lauren and Twilight galloped out of the woods towards the farm. 'How could you have –?'

'Mum! I've found Max,' Lauren interrupted her mother as Twilight slowed to a trot. 'He's stuck in the gorge.'

'Oh my goodness,' Mrs Foster said, going pale. 'The gorge!'

'He's all right,' Lauren said. 'He's on a ledge. Buddy's with him.'

'I'll ring your dad,' Mrs Foster said. 'He's in the woods.' She turned and ran back to the house.

'I'll go back there,' Lauren called after her. 'I told Max I'd get back as quickly as I could.'

Mrs Foster stopped. 'OK,' she agreed. 'If you get there before your dad, then tell Max that help will be along very soon.' She ran into the house.

'Are you OK to go back, boy?' Lauren asked Twilight.

He nodded and swung round, pulling eagerly at his bit. He suddenly seemed much livelier, almost as if he had got all his energy back. Lauren leaned forward and they cantered back into the woods again.

Lauren reached the gorge just as her dad, Tom and Hank jumped out of the pick-up truck.

'It's OK, Max,' she said, crawling to the edge. 'Dad's coming.'

'Thanks for getting help, Lauren,' murmured her brother.

'Lauren! Thank heavens you found him!' Mr Foster said,

hurrying to the edge of the gorge. Lying down on his stomach, he looked over. 'It's all right, Max,' he said. 'We'll get you up.'

Lauren watched as Tom and Hank tied one end of a long coil of rope securely around a thick oak tree and then, using it to hold on to, her dad lowered himself over the edge.

'We're ready to come back up,' he called, once he had been down there for a few minutes.

There was a bit of shouting and then Tom and Hank began to pull on the rope. Mr Foster and Max soon scrambled over the edge of the gorge.

Lauren sighed with relief as her dad hugged Max as if he were never going to let him go. 'Oh, Max! Why did you go off like that?' he said.

'I'm sorry.' Max looked close to tears again. 'I was just cross with Lauren. I'm really sorry, Dad.'

Mr Foster hugged him. 'Just don't do anything like it ever again.'

'I won't,' Max said, as Mr Foster put him down. Max looked at Lauren. 'I'm sorry I got upset with you, Lauren.'

'It's OK. I should have let you teach Buddy to fetch,' Lauren told him.

'I was being silly,' Max said. He looked at the ground. 'I'd . . . I'd like you to help me train Buddy if you want.'

Lauren smiled. 'You don't need me. You're doing fine on your own, Max. Anyway, I don't think Buddy needs much training,' she said, looking at the puppy. 'No dog could be cleverer. He was the one who found you.'

Max crouched down and hugged Buddy. 'Thanks, boy.' Buddy wagged his tail in delight.

'Come on, Max. Let's get you home,' Mr Foster said. 'The pick-up is just through the trees.' He looked at Lauren. 'Will you be OK riding back on your own?'

'I'll be fine,' she said. She waved as her dad, Hank, Tom and Max set off through the shadows. The pick-up started and Lauren listened as it drove away. Once the woods were quiet again, she took off Twilight's bridle and saddle. Then, taking a deep breath, she said the words of the Turning Spell.

Almost before the last word was out of her mouth, there was a bright purple flash and Twilight was a unicorn once more.

'Oh, Twilight,' she said, hugging him. 'Thank you for helping me.'

Twilight pushed his nose against her chest. 'I'm just glad Max is OK,' he said. 'I wish I could have used my magic to help you find him more quickly.'

'It doesn't matter now,' Lauren said. 'Your idea to use Buddy was brilliant. If you hadn't thought of that, Max might still be stuck. And anyway,' she went on quickly, 'it wasn't your fault that we couldn't use magic. It was mine. I was the one who used it all up by getting you to look at my friends.'

'You were only trying to help people,' Twilight reminded her.

'I know,' Lauren said. 'But I didn't really need magic for that. I could have seen that Mel was upset about her fractions and I should have realized that Jessica was feeling left out, and the other people I tried to help – Joanne, David, Max – well, they didn't really need my help at all.' She looked down. 'I think I just liked feeling important.'

Twilight nuzzled her. 'Don't feel bad. It turned out all right in the end.'

'Yes,' Lauren said slowly, 'thanks to you. You're the best, Twilight. Even though you were feeling really ill, you still let me ride you so that we could follow Buddy here.' She hugged him. 'How are you feeling now?'

Twilight considered the question. 'All right, actually. I don't feel tired at all.'

'Maybe it's because we've just helped Max,' Lauren suggested. 'Perhaps your powers have come back now that we've actually helped someone truly in need like the book said.'

'I'm sure that's what has happened,' Twilight said, tossing his head, 'because I feel great!' He pranced on the spot. 'Let's go flying, Lauren!'

'But it's not dark enough,' Lauren protested.

'I'll stay in the treetops,' Twilight said. He pushed her with his nose. 'Come on! I want to fly!'

Lauren couldn't resist. 'OK then!' she said, scrambling on to his back.

'I could always use my magic . . .' Twilight began teasingly.

'Not a chance!' Lauren interrupted him with a grin. 'From now on we only use your magic powers to help people who truly need help. Agreed?'

'Agreed,' Twilight said. He started to trot out of the trees and then he stopped. 'Am I really the best?' he asked, almost shyly.

Lauren nodded as she hugged him. 'The very best,' she smiled.

Magical Unicorn Secrets

Have you ever wished you could meet
a unicorn and share its magical secret?

A unicorn's horn is
filled with magic and it can do
many amazing things. The touch of a
unicorn's horn can cure any illness and
heal all wounds. And it is said
that it can turn poisoned streams
into clear, clean water.

A unicorn is an
incredible magical, graceful
creature, shaped like a horse
with a shining white coat, long
flowing mane and tail, and a
spiral horn on its forehead.

A unicorn is a gentle,
quiet creature but it can run
faster than a racehorse and be
as brave as a lion when
it needs to be.

Unicorns love all humans
and animals and are very protective.
They always tread very lightly when
they are on the ground to avoid
harming any living creature.

Unicorns can live to be
hundreds, even thousands,
of years old.

Unicorns are strict
vegetarians. They are very fond
of many kinds of berries, such
as wild strawberries
and cherries.

Some people say that
unicorns don't really exist,
but over the centuries there have
been many stories by people who
have seen them. And Lauren knows
that unicorns live in the
hearts of anyone who truly
believes in their magic.

In Chinese mythology,
the unicorn is a
creature that brings good
fortune and health.

Unicorn means 'one horn'. It comes from the Latin words *uni* (meaning 'one') and *cornu* (meaning 'horn').

A unicorn's horn is known as an 'alicorn'.

The unicorn has been found in many different cultures. The Chinese unicorn is known as a Ki-lin (pronounced 'chee-lin') and is said to have the body of a deer, with a horse's hooves and an ox's tail. And its coat is made up of five sacred Chinese colours – red, yellow, blue, white and black.

Unicorns have beautiful eyes. They are usually a deep sky blue or a misty purple, but sometimes they are chestnut brown – like Twilight's.

Baby unicorns are born with magical powers but do not know what they are straight away. They need to learn how to use their magical powers gradually.

The unicorn is a highly intelligent creature. Although one has never been caught and studied, it is known that unicorns communicate by telepathy, which means that they are able to send their thoughts and feelings to anyone they wish.

Unicorns prefer to live deep in the forest where it is quiet and peaceful. They travel by night, so there is less chance of them being seen. And for this reason, they rarely live in wide open spaces.

Unicorns often live in family groups. In each group there is an elder unicorn, a pair of unicorns, and perhaps one or two of their young. The young stay with their parents for many years before starting their own unicorn groups.

A Special Friend

Chapter One

'Lauren! Are you ready? The Parkers are here!' Mrs Foster said, looking out of the kitchen window.

'Coming!' Lauren replied. She grabbed her riding hat from the table. 'See you later, Mum.'

'Have fun!' Mrs Foster called.

'I will.' Lauren hurried out of the house to the car. Her friend Jessica sat in the back with her stepsister, Samantha. They were going to be choosing a pony and Lauren was helping them!

'Hello, Lauren,' Mr Parker said, smiling at her as she got into the back of the car.

'Hi,' Lauren said. She exchanged grins with Jessica and Samantha. They were both looking very excited.

Mr Parker started the engine. 'OK, everyone. High Meadows Farm, here we come.'

The stables were a fifteen-minute drive from Lauren's house on the outskirts of town. A signpost at the top of the farm's drive read:

High Meadows –
riding school and pony sales
Proprietor: T. Bradshaw

At the end of the drive were two red barns, an office and a large training ring.

As Mr Parker stopped the car, a woman with curly auburn hair came out of the office. 'Hi there,' she said, smiling as they piled out of the car.

'I'm Tina Bradshaw,' she said. 'So, you're looking for a pony?'

Jessica and Samantha nodded.

'I'm here to help,' said Lauren.

Tina smiled. 'Then come with me – I have plenty for you to see. I'll show you the ponies I think might be most suitable and then you can choose three or four you'd like to try out in the ring,' Tina said. She led them into the first barn and headed over to a stall where a chestnut with a white blaze was looking out. 'This is Puzzle. He's ten years old and a very good jumper. Next to him is . . .'

Lauren's brain was soon spinning with pony names. After looking at twelve ponies in the barn, Samantha and Jessica had chosen four to ride – Bullfinch, Puzzle, Lacey and Sandy. Tina saddled them and led them to the training ring.

Lauren watched as Samantha and Jessica took turns to ride the ponies around the ring. All of them looked lovely and she didn't know which one she'd choose if it were up to her.

Seeing some ponies looking over the gate of a field a little way off, Lauren wandered over to see them. There was a palomino – tan-coloured with a pale gold mane and tail – a bay and a black. Lauren stroked them and then she noticed another pony – a shaggy little dapple-grey – standing all by herself further up the field.

Lauren stared. The dapple-grey was exactly like her pony, Twilight! Although Twilight looked like an ordinary pony, he had an exciting secret. When Lauren said the words of the Turning Spell, Twilight transformed into a unicorn!

Lauren hurried round the fence. As she got closer she saw that the pony was a bit smaller and scruffier than Twilight, but otherwise just like him.

Lauren picked a handful of long grass. 'Here,' she called, holding the grass out. 'Here, girl.'

The grey mare lifted her head slightly.

'Come on,' Lauren encouraged.

The mare walked over. Stopping by the fence, she reached out and took the grass, her soft grey lips nuzzling Lauren's palm.

On her head-collar was a brass nameplate. 'Moonshine,' Lauren read out. 'Is that your name?'

The pony looked at her with sad dark eyes and a memory stirred in Lauren's mind. The very first time she had seen Twilight he had looked at her in exactly the same way. It was so weird. He and this pony were so alike they might almost be brother and sister. A thought struck Lauren and she almost gasped out loud. No, she couldn't be right . . .

'Moonshine, are . . . are you a unicorn in disguise, just like Twilight?' she whispered.

Chapter Two

Moonshine stared at Lauren. 'I know about unicorns,' Lauren said quickly. 'I have one myself.'

'Lauren!' Hearing Jessica, Lauren turned.

'Come and tell me which pony you like best,' Jessica called to her.

Lauren didn't want to leave Moonshine. 'Just a minute,' she replied. She looked at the little grey pony again. 'I won't tell anyone,' she whispered. 'Please – are you a unicorn?'

Moonshine didn't move.

'Lauren!' Jessica called impatiently.

Lauren gave up on getting Moonshine to respond. 'Coming!' She hurried back to the ring, her thoughts racing.

Jessica was riding Sandy around the ring for a second time. Seeing Lauren coming over, she called out, 'Watch how Sandy goes and then you can tell me which pony you like best.'

Lauren nodded and went to stand by Tina at the gate.

Tina smiled at her. 'I saw you talking to Moonshine just now.'

'She's lovely,' Lauren said.

Tina nodded. 'I think so too, but no one ever wants to buy her. I guess she doesn't look flashy enough. It's a shame, she's got a heart of gold. You're not looking for a pony, are you?'

Lauren shook her head regretfully. She would have loved to buy Moonshine but she knew her parents would never agree.

'Pity,' Tina sighed. 'Moonshine could do with some love. The girls who help out here prefer riding the livelier ponies and she doesn't get much attention. Oh, well.' She turned away to speak to Mr Parker.

Jessica rode over. 'So, which do you like best?' she asked eagerly.

'I like them all,' Lauren said truthfully. She watched the palomino Jessica was riding. 'Sandy's very pretty.'

'She's my favourite,' Jessica confided. 'But I think Sam likes Bullfinch.' She looked curiously at Tina. 'What were you and Tina talking about?'

'About that pony over there,' Lauren said, pointing to Moonshine who was still standing by the fence in the field.

Jessica stared. 'Isn't she sweet? She looks just like Twilight!'

Lauren nodded.

'I'll ask if we can try her out,' Jessica said.

Lauren felt a leap of excitement. If Moonshine was a unicorn and Jessica bought her, it would be brilliant! But to Lauren's disappointment, when Jessica asked, Tina shook her head.

'Moonshine will be too small for Samantha,' she told Jessica. 'She's only 12.2 hands high. You need a pony who's at least 13.2.'

'Oh,' Jessica said, looking at Lauren.

'OK, Samantha,' Mr Parker called. 'Come over here. It's decision time.'

Samantha rode over on Bullfinch.

'So which pony is it to be?' Mr Parker asked her and Jessica.

'Sandy,' Jessica said immediately.

'Bullfinch,' said Samantha at the same moment.

'Not Bullfinch,' Jessica put in quickly. 'He's too heavy and slow.'

'He's obedient and reliable,' Samantha said, patting the buckskin's neck. 'Not like Sandy. She refused when I tried to jump her.'

'She didn't with me,' Jessica said.

'Fluke,' Samantha said.

'It *wasn't*!' Jessica declared hotly.

'Sandy's only young,' Tina said. 'She's still learning about jumping. But once she gets used to jumps she should be just fine.'

'Well, I want Bullfinch,' Samantha announced.

'And I want Sandy!' Jessica frowned.

Mr Parker looked at Tina. 'I'm sorry about this – there seems to be some disagreement.'

'That's OK,' Tina said understandingly. 'Buying a pony is a big commitment. You have to be sure you're getting the right one. How about you talk it over tonight and come back tomorrow? You can try them both out again then.'

Mr Parker looked relieved. 'Are you sure that would be OK?'

Tina nodded. 'No problem.'

As soon as Lauren got home she raced upstairs to her bedroom and picked up an old blue book called *The Life of a Unicorn*. It had been given to her by Mrs Fontana, an old lady who owned a bookshop. Mrs Fontana was the only person in the world who knew about Twilight.

Sitting down, Lauren curled her legs underneath her and leafed carefully through the book, her eyes scanning the yellowing, faded pages. At last, she found what she was looking for. A picture of a little grey pony. It was a unicorn in its pony form.

She turned back a page and read the words . . .

Descendants of the two young unicorns that Noah took on to the Ark still roam the Earth today. They look like small ponies. Each of them hopes to find someone who will learn how to free them from their mortal form.

Lauren turned again to the picture of the small grey pony. Both Twilight and Moonshine were just like it. Lauren stared out of the window, frowning slightly. Was Moonshine a unicorn?

As soon as she could that evening, Lauren rushed out to find Twilight. Quickly she said the words of the Turning Spell that changed him into a unicorn:

> *'Twilight Star, Twilight Star,*
> *Twinkling high above so far.*
> *Shining light, shining bright,*
> *Will you grant my wish tonight?*
> *Let my little horse forlorn*
> *Be at last a unicorn!'*

With a bright purple flash, Twilight stood before her in his unicorn form. Lauren told him all about Moonshine.

'Well, what do you think?' Lauren asked again.

'I need to see her before I can tell,' Twilight replied.

'OK, let's fly over there now,' Lauren said. She looked up at the dusky sky. 'It's dark enough and Mum and Dad won't miss me. Mum's busy working and Dad's watching a film on TV.'

She scrambled on to Twilight's back and, with a snort, he

jumped up into the sky. Flying direct, they reached High Meadows Farm in five minutes.

Lauren scanned the ground. The only things moving seemed to be ponies. Tina and her helpers had probably gone home for the night.

'I think we can go down,' she said to Twilight. 'Look, there she is – the little grey standing all by herself.'

As Twilight swooped down, the palomino, bay and black ponies scattered to the far side of the field with snorts of alarm. But Moonshine didn't move. She stared at Twilight as if transfixed. Shaking back her mane, Moonshine slowly stepped towards Twilight, her delicate ears pricked, her hooves moving daintily on the grass. She looked so graceful with the moonlight shining on her pale coat that Lauren didn't need Twilight to tell her what he thought. Moonshine *was* a unicorn. She knew it beyond doubt.

Twilight whinnied softly. Moonshine whickered back and as she reached him, they extended their heads and touched noses.

'Unicorn,' Lauren heard Twilight murmur.

Moonshine snorted and looked at Lauren.

'What's she saying?' Lauren asked.

'She's saying she has never found anyone to be her Unicorn Friend,' Twilight said. 'It's all she's ever dreamed of.'

Lauren felt desperately sorry for the little pony. She knew that for a unicorn to be freed from its pony form, it needed to find a special person – a special person who believed in magic. Then they could share magical adventures together. She reached forward and patted Moonshine. 'You'll find someone who believes in magic. I know it.'

Lauren spoke determinedly but inside she was far from sure. *I hope I'm right*, she thought.

Moonshine bowed her head and snorted quietly.

'She says she doesn't think it will happen,' Twilight said softly.

Looking at the dejected little pony, Lauren wanted to help her more than anything else in the world. Sliding off Twilight's back, she went over and stroked Moonshine's neck to comfort her. Moonshine looked up at her, her dark eyes like deep forest pools.

Suddenly there was a change in her. Moonshine's ears pricked and she stiffened. She glanced round to the gate and then, turning back to Twilight, she snorted anxiously.

Lauren saw a look of alarm cross Twilight's face.

'Quick, Lauren,' he said. 'There's someone coming!'

Chapter Three

'Over there!' Lauren said, pointing to a nearby copse. Lauren swiftly mounted and Twilight galloped among the trees. They were only just in time. As they reached the shadows, they saw a boy walk up to the gate and climb over it. Lauren and Twilight waited in the trees, watching without being seen.

The boy headed towards Moonshine. He was skinny with untidy dark hair. He wasn't very tall but, judging by his face, Lauren guessed that he was probably about her age.

'Here, Moonshine,' she heard him say. He held out a handful of carrots. 'Here, beauty.'

Moonshine walked over to the boy. He fed her the carrots and stroked her tangled mane. 'Did you think I wasn't coming?'

Moonshine snorted.

Lauren bent low on Twilight's neck. 'Who is he?' she whispered. 'Did Moonshine say?'

'She doesn't know,' Twilight replied. 'She told me he started coming a few days ago – he's here for the summer with his family. He always brings her something to eat and just spends time talking to her and stroking her.'

Lauren watched the boy talking softly to Moonshine and suddenly made a decision. 'Wait here,' she said to Twilight as she dismounted and walked out of the trees.

The boy almost jumped out of his skin. He stared at her in surprise and then turned and began to run down the field.

'Please, wait!' Lauren called, chasing after him.

But the boy didn't stop. He raced to the gate.

'Wait!' Lauren implored him, panting for breath as she ran after him. 'I only want to talk to you!'

Glancing over his shoulder, the boy tripped over a tree root and fell. It gave Lauren the time she needed to catch up with him. She grabbed his arm.

'I wasn't doing anything!' he gasped. 'I was just talking to the pony. I wasn't hurting her, I promise.'

'I know you weren't,' Lauren said. 'It's OK.'

The boy stared at her properly for the first time. 'You're . . . you're not angry with me for feeding her?'

'No,' Lauren said in surprise. 'Of course not.' She let him go and they both stood up.

'Is it your pony?' he asked.

Lauren shook her head. 'No. She belongs to Tina, the woman who owns these stables.' She frowned. 'Who are you? What are you doing here?'

'My name's Michael,' the boy said warily. 'If Moonshine's not your pony, what are *you* doing in the field?'

Lauren didn't know what to reply. 'I . . . er . . . I was here today,' she said, 'with some friends who are buying a pony. I saw Moonshine and liked her. I thought I'd come back and visit.' At least it was half the truth.

Michael relaxed and, for the first time, he smiled at her. 'That's why I'm here too,' he confessed. 'I was exploring a few days ago and I saw Moonshine in the field. I thought she looked kind of lonely so I started to visit her. I've been coming every day. So, where do you live?' Michael asked out of curiosity.

'Not too far away,' Lauren said vaguely, thinking: *if you fly here.* 'How about you?' she asked, changing the subject.

'Me?' Michael hesitated for a moment. 'In Washington,' he replied. 'Only I'm staying in a house nearby for the summer with my mum and dad. We've done a house swap with a colleague of Jodie's . . . I mean my mum's.' He glanced at her, wondering whether to say more.

'Jodie's my adopted mum,' Michael explained after a pause. 'I haven't been with them long. My real mum died two years ago and I was put into foster care.'

Lauren didn't know what to say. 'I'm really sorry,' she stammered.

Michael gazed down. 'It's OK.'

He looked up and smiled as Moonshine walked over to him, her hooves echoing softly on the grass.

Moonshine snorted softly and rubbed her head against Michael's chest. He scratched her ears. There was silence for a moment.

'It must be strange moving to the country just for the summer,' Lauren said sympathetically.

'Yeah,' Michael admitted. 'It's hard to make new friends but at least I get to see horses – you don't see many of them in the city.' He stroked Moonshine's face. 'I stayed on a farm for a while when I was being fostered. The people there taught me to ride. I love horses.'

'Me too,' Lauren said. 'Moonshine's for sale, you know,' she added carefully. She knew she'd only just met Michael but she was already beginning to think that he might make a good Unicorn Friend.

'For sale?' Michael echoed. His face lit up briefly then faded. 'Jodie and Chris – Mum and Dad – would never buy her for me.'

'Well, ponies are expensive to buy and look after,' Lauren agreed.

Michael shook his head. 'Oh, it's not the money. It's just they're not horsey people. When I started living with them I asked if I could go to a riding school, but they didn't take me seriously. They said that I would get bored and offered to buy me a bike and a skateboard instead.'

Michael looked sadly at Moonshine. 'Jodie and Chris are really nice, but they don't understand me at all . . .' He broke off, as if he'd said too much. 'Look, I'd better go,' he muttered. 'I'll see you.'

'I'm Lauren,' Lauren said, realizing she hadn't told him her name.

'See you, Lauren,' Michael said and immediately set off at a run.

'Wait! Where do you live?' Lauren called after him.

But Michael didn't stop. Climbing over the gate, he disappeared into the darkness. Lauren stared after him until she heard a familiar whicker.

Looking round, she saw Twilight walking out from the cover of the trees.

'Michael doesn't seem very happy,' he said, joining Lauren and Moonshine.

Lauren shook her head. 'No. It must be difficult having to get used to new parents and not knowing anyone round here.'

'Apart from Moonshine,' Twilight said, nuzzling the grey pony, who nuzzled him back before staring wistfully after Michael. She whickered softly.

'Moonshine says she really likes him,' Twilight said. 'He's kind and gentle.'

'And lonely,' Lauren said. She sighed and looked at the little grey pony. Both Moonshine and Michael were so unhappy. She wished she and Twilight could help. But what could they do?

Chapter Four

The following morning, Lauren had just finished her breakfast when Mr Parker arrived. As she got into the back of his car, it was obvious that Jessica and Samantha hadn't come to an agreement on which pony they should have. They were sitting, their arms crossed, arguing with each other.

'We're getting Bullfinch,' Samantha was saying.

Jessica frowned. 'No, Sandy.'

'That's enough, you two,' Mr Parker warned. 'If you're going to quarrel, we can just forget this pony idea completely.'

Jessica and Samantha quickly stopped arguing.

There was silence for a few minutes and then Jessica looked at her sister. 'Please, Samantha,' she said quietly, 'please can we get Sandy? You heard what Tina said yesterday – she's only six, she'll learn to jump better as she gets older. And I really, really like her.'

Samantha didn't say anything.

'We could have lessons on her, couldn't we, Dad?' Jessica asked.

Mr Parker nodded. 'Definitely – in fact, I think that would be a very good idea.'

'Then I guess she would improve, and she is pretty,' Samantha admitted. She frowned. 'OK, Jess, I'll think about it.'

Jessica exchanged hopeful looks with Lauren and they travelled the rest of the way in silence.

Lauren stared out of the window. She couldn't stop thinking about Michael. She wished she knew where he lived. If she did, she could call round with Twilight. Maybe they could fly back to Moonshine's field that night and see if he visited again.

When they arrived at High Meadows Farm, they saw that Tina was lunging Sandy in the training ring.

Mr Parker stopped the car. Samantha, Jessica and Lauren jumped out and went over to the fence.

Seeing them, Tina waved. 'Hi, there,' she called, bringing the pony to a halt. 'Do you want to try Sandy and Bullfinch again?'

Jessica and Lauren looked at Samantha.

'Can we just try Sandy, please?' Samantha said to Tina.

Samantha and Jessica took it in turns to ride Sandy. She was lively but obedient and she jumped perfectly. By the time they had finished, Samantha was smiling.

'I like her,' she said, riding the pony over to the gate and halting her. 'She's been much better today.'

'And she'll continue to improve,' Tina said. 'You'll be able to do a lot with her.'

Jess turned to her dad. 'Can we have her, Dad? Please!'

'If it's all right with Sam, then OK!' Mr Parker smiled.

'Oh, thank you!' Jessica gasped. She turned to Samantha. 'And thank you for agreeing.'

'That's OK,' Samantha said happily. 'I really like her too, now I've ridden her again.'

While the girls put Sandy back in her stall, Mr Parker sorted out a price with Tina. It was arranged that she would deliver Sandy the next day.

As they turned out of the stables on to the quiet country road, something caught Lauren's eye. A boy with untidy dark hair was riding a bike up and down the drive of a nearby house. It was Michael! That must be where he was staying with his family!

She turned in her seat. Michael was cycling in circles, looking bored.

'What are you looking at?' Jessica asked, following her gaze.

'Nothing,' Lauren said quickly.

To her relief, Jessica didn't press any more. She squeezed Lauren's arm. 'It's brilliant that Samantha and I are going to keep Sandy at Mel's, isn't it? We'll be able to ride together every day.'

'Yeah, it'll be great,' Lauren agreed. Mel Cassidy was one of their friends. She lived on the farm next door to Lauren but she was away on holiday at the moment. Jessica started to talk about everything they would do together when Mel got back. Lauren listened vaguely but her thoughts were on Michael. Now she knew where he lived maybe she could ride over on Twilight to visit him. It wouldn't be that far if they went through the woods instead of going round by the roads. Michael could have a ride on Twilight. Determination filled Lauren. She was going to help him. She was going to be his friend.

It took Lauren and Twilight just over half an hour to reach Michael's house through the woods. A narrow track brought them out on to the road beside his house.

As they rode along it, Lauren heard a woman's voice coming from the garden. 'What would you like to do, Michael? We could go swimming?'

There was no reply.

'Well, how about we go to the park?' Lauren heard the woman say.

'Yeah, I guess,' Michael replied quietly. Suddenly he spoke again. 'There's a pony! I can hear a pony coming!'

He came running down the drive. Recognizing Lauren, his eyes widened.

Lauren waved. 'Hi!'

'It's . . . it's you!' Michael stammered in surprise.

Lauren grinned. 'Yes, and this is my pony, Twilight. Do you like him?'

Michael nodded, looking astonished. 'I didn't know you had a pony.'

'You left last night before I could tell you,' Lauren explained.

'He looks just like Moonshine,' Michael said.

Just then, a slim woman in her thirties with short dark hair came down the drive. *This must be Jodie*, Lauren thought, *Michael's foster mum.*

'Who are you talking to, Michael?' She stopped in surprise when she saw Twilight and Lauren.

'My name's Lauren Foster,' Lauren said in her politest voice. 'I met Michael yesterday –'

'When I went out for a walk,' Michael put in quickly.

'I thought I'd call round and say hi,' Lauren said. 'I hope you don't mind.'

'No, no, of course not,' Jodie said quickly.

'Michael told me he liked horses and I thought he might like a ride on my pony, Twilight,' Lauren said. 'We could ride in the woods.' She looked at Michael. 'If you bring your bike we could take it in turns to ride Twilight.'

Michael's face lit up. 'Great!' He turned to Jodie. 'I can, can't I?'

Jodie looked unsure. 'Well, are you sure you want to, honey?'

'Yes!' Michael exclaimed. 'Please can I?'

Jodie looked taken aback. 'Well, I guess so. He is safe, isn't he?'

'Very,' Lauren said. 'And Michael can wear my hat.'

'Well, OK then,' Jodie said. 'But don't be out too long.'

'Let's go into the woods,' Lauren said as Michael pushed his bike down the drive to join her.

'How did you know where we were staying?' Michael asked.

Lauren explained about visiting the stables with Jessica's family. 'I saw you and thought I'd come round and visit.'

They reached the main trail. Lauren stopped Twilight and dismounted. 'Here, you have a go,' she said, handing her hat to Michael.

He put it on and mounted. 'Wow!' he said, beaming.

'It's amazing to be on a pony again.'

'You can trot and canter if you like,' Lauren said. 'Twilight's very good.'

To start with, Michael just walked, but as his confidence grew he trotted and cantered. He wasn't a very experienced rider, but his hands were light on the reins and he had very good balance. At last he reined Twilight in. His eyes were shining and his cheeks were flushed. 'That was brilliant! Twilight's fantastic, Lauren!'

Lauren smiled. 'I know. I'm really lucky.'

They rode for a while longer before Michael glanced at his watch. 'I guess I should be getting back.'

They headed to his house. Jodie was standing on the front porch looking out for them. 'There you are,' she said, coming down the steps towards them. 'I was starting to worry.'

Michael looked at the ground. 'Sorry,' he mumbled.

'It's OK,' Jodie said quickly. 'You must be hungry after your ride. Would you like some cookies? I baked them this morning.'

'Yes, please,' Lauren said.

Michael just nodded.

Lauren looked at him in surprise. He had been chatty out in the woods but now he was quiet. Jodie went inside.

'Your new mum seems really nice,' Lauren said in a low voice as she tied Twilight up to the fence at the side of the house.

'She is,' Michael said. There was a flatness in his voice. 'Both she and Chris are.' He sat down on the porch steps.

Lauren heard a note of reservation in his voice. 'But . . . ?' she asked, sitting down beside him.

For a moment Michael seemed to be wondering whether to say anything more. 'But they like different things from me,' he said, with a sigh. 'And that makes it hard.'

'What do you mean?' Lauren asked curiously.

'Well, Chris is really into baseball,' Michael replied, 'and he's always suggesting we go out and practise. And Jodie's always trying to get me to go swimming. I want to please them so I just go along with them, but really I just want to be with horses.'

'What do they say when you ask if you can go riding?' Lauren said.

Michael shrugged. 'I don't really ask. I did once or twice at the beginning but not any more.'

'Why not?' Lauren demanded in surprise.

'I want to make them happy,' Michael said softly. 'I want them to be glad they adopted me . . .'

He broke off as Jodie came out of the house with a tray of drinks and chocolate-chip cookies.

'Here we are,' she said cheerfully, putting the tray down on a table on the porch. 'Have a cookie, Lauren.'

'Thank you,' Lauren said.

Jodie smiled. 'You know, I'm really pleased Michael's made a friend,' she said, sitting down on the steps too. 'What sort of things do you and your friends do in the holidays, Lauren?'

'We go to the creek and we go round to each other's houses, but most of all we ride,' Lauren said. 'Most of my friends have ponies.'

Jodie frowned. 'Really? Goodness. Things are different in the country. I grew up in the city. None of my friends ever rode.'

'Maybe Michael could start to ride while you're here,' Lauren suggested hopefully.

'Oh, I'm not sure,' Jodie said doubtfully. 'You'd probably find it a bit boring, wouldn't you, Michael?'

'No!' Michael said, looking up quickly. 'I'd love to go riding.'

Lauren's eyes suddenly widened. She'd just had a brilliant idea!

Chapter Five

'There are stables just round the corner from here,' Lauren burst out, looking at Jodie. 'Maybe Michael could help out there for the summer. He'd get to know people and he could be with horses.'

'That would be amazing!' Michael gasped. 'Can I?' he begged Jodie. 'Can I, please?'

Jodie raised her eyebrows. 'You wouldn't really want to, would you?'

'Yes,' Michael said. 'I'd love to.'

'Well, I suppose I *could* speak to the owner,' Jodie said.

Michael jumped up. 'Now?' he asked eagerly.

Jodie looked at him in amazement. 'You *are* keen. Well, OK. If it means that much to you then we can go and ask right away.' She finished her drink. 'I'll just lock the house and get my bag.'

Tina was leading Puzzle in from the field when Lauren arrived with Michael and Jodie. Jodie explained what they had come round for.

'Michael likes the idea of helping out,' she said to Tina. 'Do you let children do that?'

'Yes,' Tina replied. 'I usually have at least five or six of them helping me in exchange for rides. At the moment several are away at summer camp. I could do with another pair of hands.' She looked at Michael. 'The trouble is, you're younger than most of my helpers and I won't be able to offer you many rides. I think a lot of the ponies will be too strong for you.'

'That's OK,' Michael said quickly. 'I'd be happy just to help.'

Twilight suddenly lifted his head and neighed. From the field by the car park came an answering whinny. Tina looked round. Moonshine was standing at the gate, staring at them.

She scratched her head. 'I suppose there's always Moonshine,' she said. 'She's very quiet. You could ride her, Michael.'

'Yes, please!' Michael said. He looked at Lauren, his eyes shining.

'OK then,' Tina said. 'It's settled. You come and help me with the yard chores and you can ride Moonshine in exchange.'

'And can I groom her and clean her tack?' Michael asked eagerly.

Tina smiled at his enthusiasm. 'As much as you like.'

Lauren was desperate to talk to Twilight about the good news. She couldn't wait until that evening and so on the way home, she turned him down an overgrown path that led to a hidden glade in the woods.

Twilight walked forward eagerly, pushing his way through the overhanging branches. At last, the path opened out into the sunny clearing. The grass was springy and scattered with purple flowers. Golden butterflies fluttered through the warm, sweet-scented air. It was the most secret place Lauren knew.

She said the Turning Spell.

'So, what do you think?' she asked, as soon as the purple flash faded and Twilight was standing in front of her in his unicorn form.

'It's a wonderful idea,' Twilight said. 'Moonshine will love having someone to look after her each day.'

'And Michael will love helping with all the ponies,' Lauren said.

Twilight nodded. 'He would make a very good Unicorn Friend.'

'I know,' Lauren agreed. 'But I guess Moonshine's just going to have to wait for someone else to come along. Michael's only here for another five weeks, so he probably won't have time to find out that she's a unicorn.'

'Unless we help him,' Twilight said thoughtfully.

Lauren frowned. 'But we can't, Twilight. You know

Unicorn Friends have to find out the truth about their unicorn by themselves. That's why Mrs Fontana could only hint that you were a unicorn when I got you. We can't tell Michael. If he's going to be a Unicorn Friend, he has to believe in magic enough to try the spell without knowing whether it will work.'

Twilight nodded. 'I know, and I didn't mean that we should tell him everything, but couldn't we sort of *help* him find out the truth?'

'I guess so,' Lauren said slowly. A thought struck her. 'But if he does find out, what will happen when he has to leave Moonshine at the end of the summer? It will be awful for him.'

'But isn't it better he has five weeks as a Unicorn Friend than none?' Twilight pointed out.

Lauren hesitated. She wasn't sure. It was going to be hard enough for Michael to leave Moonshine at the end of the summer. Surely it would be a hundred times worse if he had to leave her knowing she was a unicorn?

'I don't know,' she said uncertainly. She twisted her fingers in Twilight's mane and wondered how she would feel if she had to leave Twilight. *I couldn't bear it*, she thought.

But what if she had never known about his unicorn powers? Not known what it was like to fly through the starry skies, to feel the wind against her face and Twilight's warm back beneath her? Not even having the memories . . . No, that would be even worse.

Twilight nuzzled her. 'What does your heart say, Lauren?'

Lauren hesitated. Yes, it would be dreadful for Michael to have to leave Moonshine at the end of the summer but, like Twilight had said, surely it was better that he did that instead of never knowing the truth. 'My heart says that we should help him,' she said slowly.

'Well, I think that too,' Twilight said. 'So let's do it!'

'OK,' she agreed.

As she spoke, she felt a weight drop off her shoulders. She was sure that they were doing the right thing. They should help Michael. The only question was, *how were they going to do it?*

Even though Lauren thought about it all night, by the time she rode Twilight to Tina's the next morning she hadn't come up with an answer. Michael was riding Moonshine in the ring when she arrived. Moonshine was cantering eagerly, her ears pricked.

Michael saw them. 'Hi there,' he called.

'Moonshine's looking good,' Lauren said.

Michael bent down and hugged Moonshine's neck. 'She's brilliant.'

Tina came up the yard. Seeing Lauren, she smiled. 'Hello. Come to visit?'

Lauren nodded. 'You don't mind, do you?'

'Not at all,' Tina said. She looked at Michael. 'That's probably enough ring-work for Moonshine today. Why don't you go out into the woods for a short ride?'

'OK,' Michael said eagerly.

He rode out of the yard with Lauren. 'So, are you enjoying helping Tina?' she asked.

'It's brilliant,' Michael said, his face glowing. 'I've mucked out five stables already this morning. This is going to be the best holiday ever.'

Lauren stroked Twilight. Michael's holiday would be even better if he knew about Moonshine. But how could she help him? She couldn't just start talking about unicorns out of the blue – he'd think she was crazy.

Beside her, Michael patted Moonshine's neck. 'You know, I'm sure Moonshine understands me when I talk to her,' he said. 'It's the way she looks at me. Like she's smarter than other ponies.' He laughed, sounding suddenly embarrassed. 'I guess that sounds really dumb.'

'No, it doesn't,' Lauren said. 'I know what you mean. Twilight's the same. It's like they're different from other ponies.'

She glanced quickly at Michael. Maybe this was her chance to say something more. But what could she say? Before she could think of anything, Michael had pushed Moonshine on.

'Come on, let's canter!' he called.

Twilight jumped forward eagerly.

Lauren had no choice but to let him race after the little grey mare. She felt a wave of frustration at the wasted chance. Michael would be a perfect Unicorn Friend if only he would try the spell. But how did she get him to do that? Maybe if she had lots of time she could think of a way, but in just five weeks Michael would be going back to the city.

I'll come up with something, Lauren thought, crouching low against Twilight's neck as he cantered along the path. *I just have to.*

Chapter Six

A week passed by but Lauren didn't get any further in helping Michael work out Moonshine's secret. It was so frustrating. The more she saw him with Moonshine, and realized how much he loved the pony, the more she wanted him to be Moonshine's Unicorn Friend. But she just couldn't think of how to help him find out the truth.

On Saturday, Michael came round to her house and they went down to the creek with Jessica and Samantha. They took it in turns to ride Twilight and Sandy. When they got back to her house they brushed Twilight down and then went up to Lauren's bedroom.

'I like your room,' Michael said, looking admiringly at the horse posters Lauren had stuck on the walls. He went over to the window. 'Hey, you can see Twilight's paddock from here.' Lauren's unicorn book was lying open on the window seat. Michael picked it up and started to leaf through the pages. 'Wow! This book looks interesting.'

Lauren's heart leapt. Of course! The book had all the information Michael needed.

Michael turned the first page. 'Look at this pony! It looks just like Twilight and Moonshine.'

'It's a picture of what unicorns look like when they're disguised,' Lauren said.

'What do you mean?' Michael asked, looking round at her.

And suddenly Lauren knew as clearly as anything what she had to do. 'Read the book and it'll tell you,' she told him. 'You can borrow it for the holidays.'

Michael looked surprised. 'Are you sure?'

Lauren nodded. She loved the book and didn't want to let it go – even for a few weeks – but she was sure that it was the only way that Michael was going to learn about unicorns.

'OK, thanks,' he said, looking really pleased.

'Lauren!' Mrs Foster called up the stairs. 'Michael's mum is here.'

'We'd better go,' Lauren said. They went downstairs. Jodie was in the kitchen.

'Hi, honey,' she said, as Michael came in. 'Have you had a good day?'

Michael's eyes shone. 'It's been great! We rode to the creek with Lauren's friends, Jessica and Samantha, and we had a picnic and we swam.'

'That sounds fun,' Jodie said.

'It was fantastic!' Michael said. He looked round. 'I left my bag in your tack room, Lauren. Can I go and get it?'

'Sure,' Lauren said.

Michael put the unicorn book down on the table and ran outside. Jodie shook her head. 'I just can't believe the change in him since we moved out to the country for the summer,' she said to Mrs Foster. 'He used to be so quiet, but now he talks all the time – although only about horses.'

Mrs Foster laughed. 'That sounds very familiar. Is he going to carry on riding when you return to the city?'

'We'll see,' Jodie replied. 'Kids in the city don't really ride.'

Lauren looked at her mum. 'I used to ride lots when we lived in the city, didn't I, Mum?'

Mrs Foster nodded. 'We only moved here at Easter,' she explained to Jodie. 'Before then, Lauren used to ride every weekend. I know it's not so easy but there are riding schools and kids who ride. It's a good hobby – the children learn responsibility and have fun at the same time.'

Jodie looked surprised. 'Oh, I see.'

Michael came back in. 'I've got it,' he said, waving his bag. He started to put the book carefully inside. 'Thanks for having me round, Mrs Foster.'

'It's a pleasure,' Mrs Foster replied.

'What have you got there?' Jodie asked Michael, looking at the book.

'Lauren's lent it to me,' Michael answered. 'It's a book about unicorns.'

Lauren sensed her mum glance quickly at her. Her mum knew that the unicorn book was one of the most precious things Lauren owned.

'Well, thank you very much, Lauren,' Jodie said. 'I'm sure Michael will take very good care of it.'

Lauren nodded and she and her mum saw Jodie and Michael to their car.

'So?' her mum said quietly to her as they waved them off.

'So?' Lauren said, but she knew what her mum was getting at.

'The book,' Mrs Foster said, looking at her.

'You love that book, Lauren. I'm surprised you're letting it out of your sight.'

'I know,' Lauren said. 'But Michael was looking at it today and he really liked it and . . .' she hesitated, 'and I wanted to lend it to him for the summer.'

Her mum looked at her for a moment. Then she smiled. 'There's a lot of good in you, Lauren Foster,' she said, hugging her. 'I'm proud you're my daughter.' She kissed Lauren's hair.

'Mum!' Lauren protested, but she felt a warm glow inside.

★

As Lauren rode Twilight over to High Meadows Farm early the next morning, she said, 'I wonder if Michael read the book last night.' A thought struck her. 'What if he doesn't believe it? I had the book for ages before I tried turning you into a unicorn, Twilight.' She thought back to that time. 'It was only when I saw the moonflowers in the secret glade that I started to wonder if the spell might actually work,' she said.

Twilight stopped dead.

'What's wrong?' Lauren said.

To her surprise, Twilight turned round and started heading back down the track. 'What are you doing?' Lauren asked in astonishment.

Twilight broke into a trot. Lauren quickly loosened the reins. It was clear he'd had an idea about something, although she didn't know what. She let him go where he wanted.

He trotted for about two minutes down the path, finally halting by the overgrown trail that led to the secret glade.

As soon as they entered the glade, he plunged his head down to the ground.

'You came here because you wanted to eat some grass?' Lauren said in surprise. Twilight stamped his hoof and she suddenly realized that he wasn't eating. He was nudging a moonflower with his nose.

Her eyes widened as she finally understood. 'You think we should take a moonflower to Michael?'

Twilight nodded.

'It's a brilliant idea!' Lauren said. 'He probably just thinks they're made-up flowers in the book, but if I give one to him he'll see that they really exist and maybe it'll make him try the spell.' She jumped off and picked a flower.

Twilight tossed his head as if to say, *That's what I thought all along.* Putting the flower in her pocket, Lauren remounted and they carried on their way.

★

Moonshine was tied up in the yard at High Meadows Farm. Lauren noticed how much better she was looking. Her coat was now sleek and grey and her mane and tail were silky.

Michael came out of a barn with a wheelbarrow. He was deep in thought.

'Hi,' Lauren called.

Michael looked up. 'Oh . . . hi.'

'Are you free to go for a ride?' Lauren asked.

'I've got another two stalls to muck out first,' Michael said. 'But then I can.'

Lauren dismounted. 'I'll give you a hand.' She tied Twilight up by Moonshine and then set to work, watching Michael carefully all the time.

For a while Michael worked in silence, but at last he spoke. 'I was reading that book last night.'

Lauren glanced at him eagerly. 'What did you think?'

'It was really good.' He laughed in an embarrassed way. 'I mean, I know it's not true or anything but it's a really good story.'

Lauren remembered the flower. It was now or never. 'I brought you something from the woods.' She took the moonflower out of her jeans. The gold spots on the tip of each purple petal seemed to glow in the light of the stall.

Michael looked as if he was wondering why she had brought him a flower but then his eyes widened. 'It's a . . . it's a . . .'

'Moonflower,' Lauren murmured.

Michael's eyes flew to hers. 'They really exist?'

Lauren nodded. 'Yes, and so does the Twilight Star. It shines every night for ten minutes just after the sun sets.' She met his eyes. 'You just have to believe.'

Michael stared.

Fearing that, in a minute, she'd tell him everything, Lauren pushed the flower into his hand. 'Here, take it. I'll empty the wheelbarrow.' Before he could ask her any questions, she grabbed the handles of the wheelbarrow and pushed it out of the stall.

Michael didn't say much for the rest of the morning. He seemed to be thinking hard and even when they went out on a ride, he remained quiet. On the way home, Lauren caught him looking from Moonshine to Twilight. *Oh, please*, she thought, *try the spell tonight*.

They got back to the yard to find Jodie coming out of the office with Tina.

Seeing the surprise on Michael's face, Jodie smiled. 'Don't worry, nothing's wrong. I just thought I'd call round and see Tina and find out how you were doing.'

'And I said you were doing great,' Tina said. 'Moonshine's been like a different pony since you started looking after her, Michael.'

'So, this is Moonshine, is it?' Jodie asked, looking interested.

'Yes,' Michael answered. 'Isn't she perfect?'

Jodie stroked Moonshine. 'Oh, she is pretty.'

'She's the best,' Michael said, leaning forward and hugging the little grey pony. 'Aren't you, girl? She understands everything.'

Lauren patted Twilight's neck. If only Michael knew how true that was . . .

Chapter Seven

The next morning, Lauren was up and out of the house by nine o'clock. She was longing to see Michael.

Michael was grooming Moonshine when Lauren rode into the yard at High Meadows Farm. The little pony's coat looked even glossier and her dark eyes had a new sparkle.

'Hi,' Lauren called eagerly.

Michael swung round. 'Hello!' The word almost burst out of him. He looked very excited. 'Lauren!' he said, running over. 'I've got to tell you something! Something amazing about Moonshine. She's a –'

'Ssshh,' Lauren interrupted, quickly dismounting. 'I know.'

Michael stared at her. 'What do you mean, you know?'

Lauren looked pointedly at Twilight. He followed her gaze and his eyes widened. 'Twilight's a –'

'You mustn't tell anyone,' Lauren broke in. 'No one must know about him or Moonshine. You can't talk about it – not to anyone. It's got to be a secret.'

'But . . . but . . . ' Michael stammered.

'Remember what the book said,' Lauren reminded him.

They stared at each other for a moment.

'I can't believe it's true,' Michael said, shaking his head in wonder.

Lauren smiled. 'It is. Believe me, it is.'

Just then, Tina came out of the barn. She was showing a man and a dark-haired girl around the yard.

Lauren stiffened. 'I know that

girl. She's called Monica Corder. She's in my class at school. What's she doing here?'

Michael looked surprised. 'She and her dad are looking for a pony, I think.'

'She's not very nice,' Lauren said.

'There's nothing here,' Monica was saying loudly to her dad. 'I want a pony that's going to win things.'

'Well, how about that chestnut with the blaze?' Mr Corder said. He turned to Tina. 'You said he'd won a lot lately.'

Monica folded her arms. 'But I don't want a chestnut, I want a grey.'

'Why don't you just give him a try, Monica?' Mr Corder said.

'I guess I could,' Monica said grudgingly.

'Michael,' Tina called. 'Can you tack up Puzzle for me, please?'

Monica glanced in their direction. Seeing Lauren, she frowned in surprise. 'Lauren! What are you doing here?' she said, speaking as if Lauren had no right to be in Tina's yard. Before Lauren could reply, Monica's eyes had fallen on Moonshine. 'Hey! What's *that* pony's name?' she demanded.

'Moonshine,' Michael replied.

Monica's green gaze swept over Moonshine's soft grey coat and silky mane and tail. 'I like her,' she declared. She turned to her father. 'Dad! I like this pony. She's really pretty. I'll try her too.'

Lauren and Michael stared at each other in horror.

Mr Corder turned to Tina. 'We'll have that one saddled up too, please.'

'Well, actually,' Tina said, stepping forward, 'I've already got someone booked to see that pony later this morning. They've asked to be given first refusal on her – that means they have first choice on whether to buy her or not,' she explained to Monica. 'So although you can try her out, I have to wait and let the other people see her as well.'

Lauren stared at Tina. There were other people who wanted Moonshine? But they couldn't. Moonshine couldn't be sold! Especially not now Michael had discovered her secret.

Monica scowled. 'But I like her best.'

'I'm sorry, but that's the situation,' Tina said.

'Well, I'll try her anyway,' Monica said.

Tina turned to Michael. 'Can you tack Moonshine up as well, please, Michael?'

Michael looked totally shocked as he fetched the tack. Lauren felt awful. Poor Michael. What would he do if Moonshine was sold?

Monica mounted Moonshine. She landed with a thump in the saddle and Moonshine took a surprised step backwards.

'Walk on!' Monica said sharply, digging her heels into Moonshine's sides. When Moonshine didn't respond immediately, Monica smacked her with her riding crop. Moonshine jumped forward in alarm. Lauren glanced at Michael. His face was pale.

'Just give her time to get used to you, Monica,' Tina called, standing by the gate with Puzzle.

Monica dug her heels in again. 'Come on.'

Moonshine's walk slowed down. Monica smacked her again with her crop. 'Walk on!'

But Moonshine just got slower and slower. Although she was very good for Michael she seemed determined to be as lazy as possible for Monica.

After a circuit of the ring, Monica stopped Moonshine by the gate. 'She's a useless pony,' she said scathingly. 'She's so slow.' She dismounted. 'She's way too lazy for me.'

Lauren felt a rush of relief.

'Oh well, never mind,' Tina said cheerfully. 'I think the people who are coming later this morning will be just perfect for her.'

Lauren glanced at her. Tina didn't sound like she cared about Michael's feelings. Surely she knew how upset he was at the thought of Moonshine being sold?

'I'll try the other pony instead,' Monica said.

As she mounted Puzzle, Tina turned to Michael. 'Seeing as Moonshine's tacked up, why don't you take her out for a quick ride in the woods, Michael? The other people won't be here for a while and you can smarten her up when you get back.'

Michael nodded. Lauren realized that Tina had suggested the ride to be kind because she could see that Michael was only just managing to fight back his tears.

As they rode out of the yard, Lauren looked at him. 'I'm really sorry,' she said.

Michael stared at Moonshine's mane. 'She can't be sold,' he said in a low trembling voice.

'At least Monica didn't want her,' Lauren said, trying to cheer him up.

'And maybe she'll be just as lazy for these other people, then they won't want her either.' She leaned forward. 'Moonshine. You've got to do exactly what you did with Monica this afternoon. These people *mustn't* buy you.'

Moonshine nodded slightly.

'And maybe we can put these people off her,' Lauren said, trying to think of something. 'Tell them that she's naughty or something.'

'Yes.' Michael looked suddenly hopeful, but then his face fell. 'I won't be here. Jodie and Chris are taking me shopping later.'

'Well, I'll stay,' Lauren said. 'I'll try and think of something.'

Michael swallowed. 'I know I've got to say goodbye to Moonshine at the end of the summer but not now, especially not after finding out that she's a —'

'Ssshh!' Lauren said quickly in case there was anyone nearby in the woods who might overhear. She saw a tear fall down Michael's face. 'I'll think of something,' she said desperately. 'I promise.'

Chapter Eight

As Lauren and Michael rode back to the yard, Tina came out of a barn. 'Great, you're back. Can you brush Moonshine over and oil her hooves, Michael?'

'Did Monica buy Puzzle?' Lauren asked.

Tina shook her head. 'She didn't like him, although at least he was better behaved than Moonshine.' She walked over and patted the little grey pony next to Michael. 'I've never known you so lazy, girl. I guess you just didn't like her.'

Leaving Michael to smarten up Moonshine, Tina went to the tack room. Lauren tried desperately to think of a plan.

'I'm going to have to go in a minute,' Michael said, looking at his watch after he'd oiled Moonshine's hooves. 'Have you thought of anything, Lauren?'

She shook her head. 'Not yet.'

'What am I going to do?' he said.

Just then there was the sound of a car coming down the drive. Tina came out of the tack room. 'Ah, here are the people to see Moonshine.'

Michael and Lauren looked round at the black car.

'No it's not, Tina. It's my mum and dad,' Michael said. 'They must have decided to come and get me. We're going shopping.'

'Yes,' Tina said with a smile. 'I know.'

Lauren looked at her. There was something about the way she was smiling . . .

Michael had obviously noticed it too. He looked from Tina to his mum and dad who were parking the car. 'What . . . what's going on?' he asked.

'Yes, you're going shopping, Michael – for a

165

pony,' Tina told him.

Both Lauren and Michael stared at her.

'A pony!' Michael gasped.

Tina nodded. 'When your mum came to see me yesterday, it was to talk about buying you Moonshine. I suggested she come with your dad to see her today.'

'I . . . I don't believe it,' Michael stammered. Jodie and Chris got out of the car. Michael raced over to them. 'I'm getting a pony? I'm really getting Moonshine?' His eyes looked almost wild.

'If you want her,' Jodie said.

'Oh yes, I do! More than anything!' Michael cried.

'Then she's yours,' Chris smiled.

'But where will I keep her?' Michael burst out.

'I phoned some stables in the city and found one near home,' Jodie said. 'They have a pony club there. You'll be able to learn all sorts of things – have lessons, go in shows.'

Chris nodded. 'And they run stable management classes for the parents too, so Jodie and I will be able to learn about horses and help you.' He squeezed Michael's shoulder. 'If you want us to, of course.'

Michael looked almost lost for words. 'That . . . that would be great.' He swung round. 'Lauren! Did you hear that?'

She grinned at him. 'Yes. It's great!'

Michael grabbed hold of Jodie and Chris's hands. 'Come and see Moonshine,' he said, half pulling them up the yard.

Moonshine whickered as they got close. Michael ran over and patted her proudly. 'You're going to be mine!' he told her.

'We just want you to be happy,' Jodie said to him, smiling at his joyful face. 'It's all we've ever wanted. We only tried to get you to do things like baseball and swimming because we thought you'd enjoy them.'

'I know,' Michael said. 'It's just that I prefer horses.'

'I guess we only realized that once we saw how much you've liked coming and helping here,' Chris said. 'I mean before that you'd only mentioned riding once or twice.'

'I know.' Michael looked awkward. 'It was because you didn't seem keen on the idea when I did mention it so I stopped. I wanted to please you and do what you wanted.'

'I think we've all been trying a bit too hard,' Jodie said. 'Maybe now the three of us can really start being a family.' She walked forward and patted the little grey pony. 'Sorry, I should have said the four of us, of course. Welcome to the family, Moonshine.'

Moonshine whickered softly and Michael threw his arms round Jodie and Chris in delight. They hugged him tightly.

Lauren's thoughts were whirling. She could hardly believe that after she and Michael had been so worried things had all ended perfectly.

Tina smiled at him. 'I told you she'd be going to a perfect home, didn't I?'

Michael nodded. 'But I didn't know you meant me. I'm so lucky. She's the best pony in the world!'

Twilight snorted.

'One of the two best ponies in the world,' Michael corrected himself.

The adults laughed.

'Everyone thinks their pony is the best pony in the world,' Tina commented.

Michael grinned at Lauren. 'But in our case it's true, isn't it?'

Lauren grinned back. 'Definitely,' she said.

The night air was warm and still as Lauren and Twilight stood in the shadow of the trees waiting for Michael to visit Moonshine. Twilight bent to rub his head against his knee as a shaft of moonlight shone down through the branches and glanced off his pearly horn.

'He's coming,' Lauren whispered. 'Look.'

Twilight lifted his head. Michael was hurrying down the drive.

Moonshine was waiting by the gate. She whinnied softly, her ears pricked.

Michael climbed the gate and stood beside her, his hand on her grey neck. Lauren saw his lips move. Suddenly there was a bright purple flash and Moonshine was transformed into a unicorn. She was beautiful, her long tail swept almost to the ground and her coat gleamed like mother of pearl in the moonlight.

'What should we do?' Twilight murmured. 'Do you think we should go over and say hello?'

Lauren looked at Michael and Moonshine. They were standing only inches apart, their heads almost touching. They looked lost in their own little world.

'No,' Lauren said suddenly. 'Let's leave them.'

As she spoke, Michael got on to Moonshine's back. Moonshine turned and, pushing off with her hind legs, she cantered up into the sky. Lauren smiled, her eyes shining.

At long last Moonshine had found a true Unicorn Friend and it wasn't just for the summer. It looked like they were going to be together for a long, long time to come – just like her and Twilight.

As she turned Twilight for home, Lauren buried her face in his silvery mane. They had so many more wonderful adventures ahead of them – she couldn't wait!

Do you love magic, unicorns and fairies?

Join the sparkling

My Secret Unicorn

fan club today!

It's FREE!

You will receive a sparkle pack, including:

Stickers　　**Badge**
Membership card　　**Glittery pencil**

Plus four Linda Chapman newsletters every year,
packed full of fun, games, news and competitions.
And look out for a special card on your birthday!

How to join:

Send your name, address, date of birth* and email address (if you have one) to:

My Secret Unicorn Fan Club
Abloads Court
Sandhurst
Gloucestershire
GL2 9NG

My Secret Unicorn

Collect them all!

The Magic Spell
ISBN: 0141313412

Dreams Come True
ISBN: 0141313420

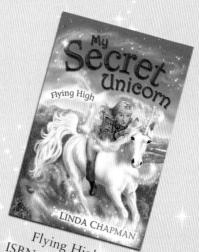

Flying High
ISBN: 0141313439

Starlight Surprise
ISBN: 0141313447

Stronger Than Magic
ISBN: 0141313455

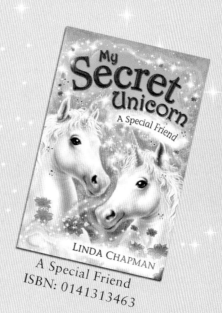

A Special Friend
ISBN: 0141313463

My Secret Unicorn

A Winter Wish
ISBN: 0141318465

A Touch of Magic
ISBN: 0141319798

Snowy Dreams
ISBN: 0141320265

Twilight Magic
ISBN: 0141320257

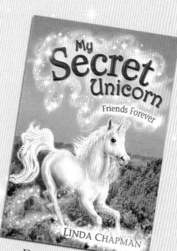

Friends Forever
ISBN: 0141320249